ALSO BY CHERI LASOTA

Immortal Codex Series

Petra, Book 1
Leander, Book 2 (Coming Soon)

Standalone Novels

Artemis Rising
Echoes in the Glass

Paradisi Exodus Series

Paradisi Chronicles Sci-Fi Universe

Paradisi Escape, Book 1
Sideris Gate, Book 2
Tenebra Sojourn, Book 3 (Coming Soon)

PETRA

IMMORTAL CODEX

BOOK I

CHERI LASOTA

COPYRIGHT

ISBN-13: 978-1544807393
ISBN-10: 1544807392

To book the author for engagements or gain permission for reprints and excerpts contact:

Cheri Lasota
www.CheriLasota.com
Cheri@CheriLasota.com

TABLE OF CONTENTS

Author's Note

You'll find a glossary of words in the back of the novel.
Just look for the foreign words in italics throughout the story.
Enjoy!

The Prima Vita

Sicily

February 21, 1723

"**M**ADAME PETRA, PLEASE FORGIVE MY BOLDNESS, BUT MAY I ASK…?" Aurelia bit her lip, hesitating, but Lady Petra Valerii was waiting, one eyebrow arched. "How many times have you died since the turn of the first millennium, my lady?" She immediately regretted asking. It was not like her to question Petra about her past—a past she had long concealed.

"Contemplating your own immortality tonight, Aurelia?" Petra asked, laughing softly as she glanced up from the pianoforte Lucius had given her last year. The lady hadn't the natural skill or interest in music that he had, but she still loved to stumble through Pietro Scarlatti's toccatas to while away the rainy Sicilian winter nights.

Tonight Aurelia had been hard at work on her encryption for hours in the *Essentiae* enclave's massive library, as she was most nights after transcribing Petra's dictation for the Immortal Codex, a secret history spanning millennia. But now her quill stood motionless in the inkwell as she gazed at her maker. Petra wore a wide contouche gown in the French style, the folds of gold shimmering in the flickering firelight as the luxuriant fabric spilled to the floor. Cobalt-blue ribbons adorned the embroidered flower design at her breast and wove deep into the strands of

1

her half-updo and the loose plait falling down her flawless neck.

Though she looked no older than eighteen, Petra had always possessed the bearing of a queen, and age had only deepened her unearthly beauty. Time had smoothed her skin as a river polishes rock. Aurelia found it impossible to look away from her stunning eyes tonight. They glowed an icy grey rimmed with black, as stones shot through with silver.

That same piercing gaze made Aurelia mute as she tried to formulate her fear into words. The Lady Petra had only been a year older than Aurelia when she first became an immortal, yet her understanding of the world, her fearlessness, her grace, far surpassed Aurelia's own meager strengths. If she hadn't spent the last few centuries writing Petra's histories of the Essentiae, she would have believed the woman a goddess sent from the heavens to save them all. In fact, the year she first met her back in Avignon, France in 1345, she *had* believed it.

"What makes you ask?" Petra prompted, her faded Roman accent a sharp contrast to Aurelia's own soft French tones. Even here at their estate in Sicily, long after their ancient beginnings, they could not escape the trappings of their pasts.

"Forgive me, Madame," she finally said, "I was remembering the last time I died. How I feared it. How much it hurt. I worry death will soon come for me again."

Petra pressed her lips together, her expression tinged with a knowing look, her gaze softening. "You know I will always bring you back."

"Yes, Madame. I know."

The lady waited a moment longer, undoubtedly wishing to ascertain if Aurelia truly believed her promise. Aurelia smiled back as she swirled the quill nervously in the inkwell.

"You still seek an answer, yes? Well, I may be cursed with near-perfect memory, but even I can't remember how many times. Though I suppose I must be nearing two thousand by now."

"The only true immortal," Aurelia murmured. Horror and awe battled for dominance in her mind. "I have often wondered what death is like for you... why you do not fear it."

"I carry the instrument of my death on a chain around my neck, Aurelia." Petra smoothed her fingers over the *ankh* amulet, an ancient Egyptian symbol of immortality, and a phial of *mortanine* poison. "Talk to me of fear, and I will tell you no one on Earth has ever feared death more. But there will likely never be another who fears it less. Death is both my curse and my gift."

"And life?"

"It is the same."

"If you did truly die someday—?"

"That cannot happen. All of you would die with me."

"Would you welcome a permanent death if it were offered? If you didn't have so many of us under your care?"

"Never."

Aurelia's eyebrows rose in surprise. "You have not once tired of life, Madame?"

"Of course, but you and Lucius anchor me here as certainly as the mountains remain standing after millennia of war and destruction."

"I am grateful, Prima Vita." Aurelia dipped her head in reverence. She hadn't called Petra by the name First Life in many long years, but it seemed fitting tonight given the dark turn her thoughts had taken.

A faint smile touched Petra's lips. "And I am honored to count you among my Essentiae, Aurelia."

"I do not mean to pry into a past you have long told me you wished never to remember again… but I have always wondered about your First *Vellessentia*."

Petra rose from the pianoforte and walked toward Aurelia's desk. "Surely you remember it is already written in the Immortal Codex. You encrypted it yourself." She swept a hand across the vast library filled with thousands of books, many of which were the codex itself. Row upon row filled the farthest section of the library, a comprehensive history of their memories, their tragedies, their triumphs, their deaths.

"I meant the First Vellessentia, when you and Lucius and Clarius were created. Should not the origin story of our bloodline take prominence in the codex?"

Aurelia's words were innocent, but they made Petra shudder and turn away.

"I'm sorry, Madame. I did not mean…" Aurelia's voice trailed into nothing as Petra paced beside a long row of codex books, lost in memory. They had all seen so many horrors throughout their lives together. That Petra would be so hesitant to tell this story made Aurelia realize how abhorrent it must be.

When a soft knock sounded on the door, Petra had wandered into the section of the library housing the Year 1 AD Codex. There were no other Essentiae histories before this first ancient book.

"Come in," Petra called, her fingers sliding down the spine of a book.

A pair of vivid brown eyes appeared as the door cracked open and Lucius entered.

"Coming to bed, my love?" he called to her after giving Aurelia a warm smile.

At first Petra did not speak. Lucius gazed at her without a word, his patience infinite. He knew her well enough to know she was lost in one of her memories.

"Aurelia has asked me for our origin story," Petra finally said, glancing at her and pointedly avoiding his penetrating gaze.

After a moment, he raised his eyebrows at Aurelia. "You ask much, Mademoiselle."

His words were not unkind, but Aurelia immediately rose and went to Petra, taking up her hands with a gentle squeeze.

"I beg forgiveness, Madame. I didn't—I should have known not to ask. I only know it is a story that has never been recorded."

Lucius's gaze shifted from all the bookshelves around the room to Petra herself. "Aurelia is right. You should tell her." He looked to Aurelia. "And you should make her. We have held onto our past long enough. To speak it out loud would relinquish its power over us."

"It's late, Aurelia," Petra said, releasing herself from the girl's grasp.

Lucius would brook no refusal. He pulled Petra to him, his arms loosely encircling her waist. "Beauty still walked alongside our horrors in those ancient days, my love," he whispered to her.

"I remember it all," Petra said, her voice lowering to match his. "It is the reason I fear to go back there."

His wide and encouraging smile was disarming even to Aurelia. He had always had this way about him. Effortless confidence, a desire to please, but a tinge of dark jealousy lingering beneath the surface—a jealousy stemming from that secret past they had hidden from Aurelia for so long.

"I'll tell you what I remember most from those days…" Lucius said, his voice playful as his fingers delicately smoothed a stray strand of hair from Petra's forehead.

> "Come to me now and loosen me
> from blunt agony. Labor
> and fill my heart with fire. Stand by me
> and be my ally."

Petra's growing smile turned into a kiss as Aurelia politely backed away from them.

"Leave it to you to quote Sappho to tempt me back to Tivoli," Petra whispered, kissing Lucius once more.

"I am not tired, Madame," Aurelia said, risking the Prima Vita's ire—out of curiosity or foolishness, she did not know. "I would be happy to transcribe any stories you might wish to share tonight."

Lucius smiled once more, and Petra finally gave an imperceptible nod.

"Thank you, Madame." Aurelia rushed to her desk, flipped to a new page in the codex she was working in, and held her quill poised for a long night ahead.

"Shouldn't you start a new book?" Lucius asked.

Aurelia shook her head. "I can add it to a new book later. Is the story that long?"

Lucius let out a laugh and grinned as Petra suppressed a smile of her own.

"Yes. As you may have noticed"—he brought Petra's hand up to his lips and kissed it—"immortality takes a fair amount of time."

PART I

2 BC

The Villa di Avidus

The Birth

Tivoli

July 13, 2 BC

ROUGH HANDS SHOOK PETRA'S SHOULDERS HARD, BUT HER TEAR-CAKED eyelids wouldn't open.

"Wake up, girl, or you won't live through the night."

Rubbing last night's dust and sorrow from her eyes, Petra made out the hulking shape of Silvipor, the favorite house slave of her Master Clarius Valerius Avidus, in the room she shared with all the other slave women.

The way the long shadows crossed Silvipor's weary, pock-marked face brought it all back to her. No. She must not let the images come. They fought her, as she had fought with her master before all was lost yesterday. Petra concentrated on the flash of Silvipor's eyes in the moonlight, willing the memories away.

"The master's baby has nearly come," Silvipor whispered.

"I don't care."

The whites of his eyes shone as he glanced at the other sleeping slaves around them. "You must not say such things."

She drew away from him and pressed her lips into a hard line. The heat of her rage battled with a wave of shivers from the cool night air pouring in from the open window.

"The mistress was screaming when I left the villa. She thinks the baby is turned inside her. The master says you must come. You have to deliver the child now your mother has been taken by the gods."

"No!" Petra shouted, ignoring the other slaves waking around them. "Even the gods wouldn't make me do that."

Silvipor shook his head. "The gods would see you dead if you do not."

"Then I will die."

The visions hit Petra again, so rich with detail she tasted last night's dust in her mouth, smelled the fear in her mother Diantha's cracking voice. Petra had followed them out into the villa's inner courtyard as her mother stumbled behind the master, his grip on the chain around Diantha's neck as hard as the iron it was made from. The master heeded no pleas for mercy. With a flick of his wrist, he cut Diantha's throat, her soundless scream deafening as Petra collapsed before her mother's prone body. Blood splashed onto the mosaics as the dagger flashed in the fading light of the setting sun. Diantha gasped for one last breath that would never come again.

All this butchery because her mother refused to allow him to harm his wife with the witless folk cures advised by the neighboring village midwife: a bloodied, rotten hyena's foot pressed to the abdomen and a potion of goose semen. What foolish nonsense! It was not the Greek way. Not her mother's way. She had had more sense in one hand than these rural midwives had in their whole bodies.

A palm covered Petra's mouth, but it wasn't Silvipor. It was her *Lucipor*.

"Be still." The fear lacing Lucipor's whisper made her realize she was shaking again. He had never once stepped foot in the women's slave quarters. The punishment would be severe if Master Clarius found out. She glanced at Silvipor, but now he stood waiting outside the door on the path leading up to the master's house.

"Lucipor," she breathed into his mouth, when his palm was replaced by his lips against hers. As he pulled back, she looked into his shadowed eyes, wishing she could see their true color: a deep brown as fine as the richest soil in all of Italy. But the faded colors of night hid the details of his beautiful face from her. "The master is asking for me. What should I do?"

"You must go. You must do what the master asks of you." His fingers touched the bronze slave collar at her neck to remind her of her place.

"You forget I was not always a slave, Lucipor," she whispered, drawing attention to his name, a combination of slave boy and their master's *praenomen*. "I remember what it felt like to be free back in Greece before the Roman army stole us from our homes."

"You are not free now."

"I can be again."

"Not that way. Any way but that, Petra."

"I cannot do what you ask——"

Lucipor stopped her words with a kiss, but she pushed him away, glaring at him, willing him to understand.

"I will kill him if I see him again."

Lucipor shook his head. "I know you have a will of iron, Petra, but please listen to me. Your mother was a mother to me too. Losing you both would…" He let his words fade into another kiss, and this time she did not fight him. This time she kissed him back, knowing it would likely be the last time she would feel the touch of him. They had had so little time. Merely a few months of stolen moments, of shy looks, of hands touching in the shadows when the master's back was turned.

Lucipor pulled away and held her head in his hands. "Your kiss was a farewell, Petra." His voice broke as he said the words.

"If you are ever freed, find out where Master Clarius sold my father. Take care of him? He will need you."

"Don't be foolish. Your father needs you. Live for him." His thumb slid down her cheek. "Live for me."

"I will do what I must. If it means I die in revenge of my mother's murder, then so be it."

Petra almost felt the slice of the blade the master had slid cleanly through her mother's neck. Had it only been just last night? Her anger surged, and she pulled back from Lucipor.

Master Clarius Avidus commanded loyalty at the end of a whip. If he did not get it, he would fly into a rage. At twenty-five, he was young in mind if not in body—too young to take control over his father Lucius Valerius Avidus's villa and vast *latifundia* filled with endless wheat fields. But his father, a man they had all loved and respected, had died late last year of the fever. A fair master and *pater* he was, and a kind one.

Clarius was the opposite; his rage was so uncontrollable even his father refused him as he lay dying. Young Clarius's mercurial nature had left him unwilling to reconcile with his father at the bitter end. Everything had changed that day, and the once idyllic life at the Villa di Avidus turned into misery. It was no worse a life than those lived by other slaves in the vast Roman Republic, which stretched all the way from Hispania to Asiana. Many suffered a far worse fate. She had heard rumors of slave revolts in previous decades led by Spartacus somewhere south of Rome, and she often wondered if she would have had the courage to join them had she been born a man. She was glad Lucipor had never talked of escape. She could not have born Clarius's cruelties without him by her side.

"Go, Petra," Lucipor said. "Be silent. Do good work. And come back to me. Don't do this for the master. Do it for his father and his father's grandchild. Please."

She did not answer, only turned to slip on her tunic and tie her long black hair away from her face. She glanced at him from time to time, trying to memorize his face. Tonight, his dark brown hair was curled behind his ears but, as always, a few strands had fallen loose to tumble down his gaunt cheeks. His shoulders, once thin, were now broad and wide, perfect for enveloping her in an all-consuming embrace.

Many months ago, the master had ridden away in his chariot all in a rage. The horses charged through the fields, unable to stop. The master had not seen her crouched over near the road leading away from the villa, picking grapes from the vines alongside Lucipor. So focused had Petra been on her own thoughts, her own daydreams of soaking in a pool of cool water, she hadn't noticed in time. Lucipor was laboring behind her as she dawdled, but he tossed the fruit to the ground and caught her around the waist, whipping her back against his body as the master's horses galloped by no more than an arm's length away.

The shock of the moment did nothing to make her forget the feel of Lucipor's arms around her. She had always thought him thin, short, gaunt. But as his chin hovered over the top of her head and his muscled arms surrounded hers, Petra realized Lucipor had grown into a man. She asked him later that day how old he was. He said he couldn't remember, but he figured he was probably at least eighteen, the same as she was. It only took a single moment—a single touch—and then her daydreams were filled with him. It wasn't just her in the cool pool of water. Lucipor was there now, with those same strong arms surrounding her.

Before Petra left the slave quarters, Lucipor's arms came around her again. He held her hard against him, muscles taut. Petra lifted her face up to his last kiss, and out of the corner of her eye, she saw one of the little slave girls wake up and stare wide-eyed up at them.

Let the girl stare, Petra thought. Let the slaves whisper. I defy them all.

"Remember our Sappho, Petra?" Lucipor whispered. "Labor and fill my heart with fire. Stand by me and be my ally."

"Te amo," Petra said a little too loudly, her recklessness growing along with her anger.

"Then love me enough to live."

"Come, girl," Silvipor whispered harshly from across the room, his shadow trailing across the beds of snoring slave women as he stood in the moonlight pouring in through the open doorway.

She moved to follow him, but Lucipor grabbed her arm, his eyes piercing her even in the half-dark.

"Promise me," he said.

Petra nodded, but only so he would release her. She had no intention of keeping her word. He could not ask this of her. No one could.

Ever vigilant, Silvipor licked his fingers and smoothed back the frizzy strands of dark brown hair at her temples when she reached him.

"Your eyes are puffy," he said gruffly.

"Let the master see my grief."

"You forget it was your own mother who refused to do as he commanded. He was well within his rights."

"He murdered her."

"It is the way of it, girl." His tone brooked no further insolence.

As they rushed along the rocky path toward the master's quarters, Petra was glad she had donned her second tunic. A chill had descended into the valley on this windless night. They entered through the servants' *posticum* at the side of the main house.

"Wait, I need to fetch my mother's supplies." As Silvipor grunted in irritation, his scowl reminding her of an angry bear, Petra hurried into one of the tiny rooms along the side of the house where the slaves' cleaning supplies were kept. There was no one in the room, so she quickly knelt before the tiny trunk where her mother kept medical instruments and midwifery tools. She would take the supplies with her, of course, but she was looking for something else.

Beneath all of the other tools, she found the bottle she sought. The phial was unmarked and the liquid inside was clear. It came from the red mortanine flowers growing along the banks of a tiny island in the lake beyond the master's fields. Her mother discovered it was an effective rat poison years before.

With shaking hands, Petra slipped the phial into her mother's bag and followed Silvipor out of the room. Every house servant they passed upon entering the villa rushed them along with either a gesture or a word until, eventually, Petra heard the screams.

She had often accompanied her mother, Diantha, on her midwifery rounds among the Avidus slaves and servants as well as those in neighboring villas throughout the countryside, but while the master had once trusted her mother's skills before he took her life, he had forbidden Petra to assist in his child's birth. Petra's mother was renowned for her skill, much of which her own mother had taught her back in Corinth, Greece, before

Roman soldiers had taken her whole family as slaves. Diantha had helped the slave women deliver their babies. In fact, she had helped deliver the master himself before Petra was born.

As little as she knew about midwifery, Petra could tell by the sheer terror lacing Constantia Avidus's screams something had gone horribly wrong. Petra assumed it was a breech baby, but her mother had never let her deliver one before. Even if she did help them, and Clarius's wife and child died anyway, Petra knew he would kill her purely out of vengeance.

The master did not care for his wife, but he remained loyal to her. Such a man could never love. Not truly. Not the kind of love she and Lucipor felt. The kind that turned hearts into liquid, the kind that melted a gaze into moonlight. Petra said a prayer to Venus and Artemis, the Roman and Greek goddesses of fertility, though why she could not say. She believed in her mother's Greek gods and goddesses—not those of her masters. This child's delivery meant only another master to serve, and who was to say he wouldn't be as cruel as Clarius when he came of age? She rubbed the smooth glass of the phial within the supply bag and slipped into the mistress's quarters. The master was there, his back turned to her, and Petra thought it strange. Birthing was women's work. Then again, he had killed his midwife, so who was left but inexperienced slaves and servants?

Constantia was looking up at him with terror in her eyes as he held the backs of his fingers to her perspiring temple. Rarely had Petra seen him showing such tenderness toward her. Petra had expected him to be raging at Constantia for putting his baby at risk, or at least the servants for not serving him fast enough. It was his way. And, yet, both he and his wife were locked together in this silent moment of anguish. Petra wanted to hate Clarius for evoking this strange sense of pity for them, but she could not. She squeezed her eyes shut, shook her head, and it was then Constantia noticed her.

"Come here, girl," Constantia said, her voice cracked and weakened from exhaustion. Petra knew she had been in labor for at least a day already.

"Yes, *Era* Constantia." Petra locked eyes with the woman, avoiding Clarius's gaze burning a hole in her head as she passed him by. At one point, she thought he would reach out and strike her, but instead, he stood like a stone in the center of the room, his growing anger at her presence as tangible as the child who would not come from his wife's womb. It must have been Constantia who called for her and not the master.

Petra knew what was in his mind. He wished her dead and at the same time hoped she would keep his child alive. Petra's heart raced in time with her breathing. The skin along the surface of her arms tingled with fear.

"The baby is turned, girl. I can feel it." Constantia grabbed her arm hard, but Petra did not cry out. She set the tools aside and moved around to the other side of the bed so she could gauge how far along the woman was. Petra tried to remember her mother's teachings, but all her thoughts were focused on one thing: the mortanine poison.

"What's wrong with her, girl?" the master demanded. "What do you see?"

Petra avoided his gaze, knowing she would not be able to stop herself from spitting in his face. She took stock of the contents of the room. The house slaves had brought in all the necessary items. There was a hard couch for the mother's resting periods between labor pains and a softer couch for resting after the birth. Next to the hard couch where Constantia lay stood Diantha's birthing chair, a tool of her trade she had carried with her since their days in Greece. It offered strong support to the mother's back and a crescent-shaped opening in the seat through which the child would eventually pass.

On a nearby table lay a small *amphora* of olive oil for massaging the belly as well as bottles of salt and honey to scrub mucous from the baby's skin after birth. Warm water filled a bowl and cloth strips were stacked at the ready.

All this was useless in the end. A single glance at the poorly presenting cervix and the shocking amount of blood loss told Petra everything she needed to know. This woman would likely die and the baby along with her if it were not stillborn already. Perhaps Diantha could have saved them with her decades of experience, but Petra had never even seen a breech birth, much less delivered one. To confirm it, she patted Constantia's thigh to have her open wider and examined her. She probed inside gently and realized what she felt was only one of the baby's feet. She couldn't locate the other foot at all. Blood had soaked the bed and covered the poor woman's legs.

Petra did not look at the master as she finally responded to his question. "The baby is breech."

Constantia moaned at the confirmation of her suspicions. "It's too much, Clarius. I must have a tonic for the pain." She leaned onto her side with a hand to her belly as the contractions started again.

"Give her something, girl!" the master shouted with a dismissive wave of his hand.

Petra hesitated. This was the moment, when she would choose life or death: for Constantia, for the baby… for herself.

15

Faced with this woman's agony, she poured through the supply bag looking for anything to ease her pain. It wasn't truly Constantia and this baby she wanted to suffer—it was the master himself. She knew the mother and baby would die whether she helped or not. The poison would end her suffering faster if nothing else.

"Do it now!" Desperation tinged Clarius's angry shout, as his wife's contractions reached a fever pitch. He grabbed the bag and dumped it out all over the couch beside his wife, who was screaming from the pain. He threw the instruments to the floor, recklessly sifting through the contents for something useful.

"I have no true tonic," Petra said evenly.

"Then what exactly is in this phial here, girl?" Clarius held up the mortanine poison, and Petra resisted the overwhelming urge to snatch it back from him.

"I—I don't know what it's for or…," Petra said, backing away from the master, "…or if it would harm the baby."

"Give!" was all Constantia could get out before a contraction left her speechless.

Petra knew the woman was in excruciating pain. Wouldn't it be a mercy to give her a quicker release? Petra looked up at Clarius, then, an overarching revenge filling her chest, shivers and heat vying for dominance inside the layers of her skin.

The master took one last look at the liquid in the phial and handed it to his wife. The woman took it, the greed of relief shining in her eyes.

"No!" Petra screamed. Then her vision blurred into a vision of her mother out in the midday dust as the blood poured from her open neck and her body crumpled into the dirt at the master's feet. *Mother… Mother, please come back to me…*

The vision faded into darkness. Petra shook her whole body, trying to rid herself of the images of death, of murder. When she opened her mind to reality once more, death looked out through Constantia's eyes as she clutched the half-empty phial in her trembling fist.

Petra stared as a strange expression came over the woman's face, as she began to understand something was horribly wrong. She looked straight at Clarius as he slowly turned to stare at her, confusion and anger flashing in his expression.

"Now we are even, master." Her voice was steady but held none of the real contempt she wanted to feel. She felt empty, hollow, ashamed.

It took him only a moment to realize what she meant, and only a moment more to strike her senseless.

Petra ended up against the wall in the corner of the room, her jaw on fire, blood filling her mouth from a gash the master had ripped open in her lip, her ears ringing. She kept her eyes closed, waiting... for what, she knew not. Would it be a dagger? A whip? Or perhaps stones or a crucifixion.

The master's voice was far away. He was shouting, yes, but not at her. There was something about the baby. He wanted it out. The woman was screaming as if death was only moments away. Petra remembered: it was. Constantia was in her death throes now. At any moment, it would all be over. And, in a few moments more, it would all be over for her too.

Strange noises came from the bed. The woman was hysterical. No, no, it was the master himself, grunting with effort, shouting as though a madness had entered him. Petra didn't understand a word, but she had heard the sounds before. She dared to look up. The master was ripping the dead child from its mother's womb. Blood streamed from Constantia's corpse, covering Clarius's arms and the pale cloths surrounding her.

Petra brought her hand up to her mouth, covering the cry that would not come. The master stared at the blue-skinned infant in his hands, shaking the boy until his head lolled back against his mother's leg.

"My son, my son..." the master said over and over, as if by saying the words he could will the boy back to life.

Petra watched all of this almost unseeing. Somewhere in the recesses of her mind she remembered she was the architect of this bloody scene. Soon, the master would have his own revenge and hasten her own inevitable end.

The smell of sickness and blood hovered thick in the air. Petra finally noticed the throng of horrified servants who had gathered in the hallway. They dared not enter. They stared at her, accusation and shock burning in their eyes. Only one wore an expression of relief. It was Constantia's personal slave, the young girl who could never please her mistress, no matter how hard she tried. The girl was glad, at least, the woman was gone. Petra fixed her mind upon the slave girl, clinging to her as if she were a hand outstretched to save her from drowning.

The master laid the boy down at last and looked at his wife's face with a finality. With a hand on her bloodied leg, Clarius finally looked full and long at Petra. She stared back at him, and they remained locked in mutual hatred for what seemed an eternity. She realized, then, even if she did somehow escape death this day, that hatred would never dissipate, never die.

When the master finally spoke, his voice was dispassionate. "I am going to revel in your death, slave girl. When it is done, I will put your head on a pike for all the slaves to see. I will not order you down until the birds have pecked your skull clean. I will burn your bones until there is nothing left of you but ash and all memory of you is gone. Then, and only then, will we be even."

II

The Master

July 13, 2 BC

PETRA HEARD THE MASTER'S THREAT AS IF THROUGH A DREAM. SHE DID not see him through her hazy vision. She saw only Lucipor before her, his eyes willing her not to look away from him. He said the words again, only this time they were a whisper.

Love me enough to live…

I couldn't do it, Lucipor. I couldn't let this go.

The master rose from the bed. She knew because his shadow fell across her body as she crouched against the wall.

Clarius took hold of her wrist and yanked her up to her feet, banishing the comforting image of Lucipor's beautiful, soft eyes. She did not fight, unsure if it would prolong a more painful death or quicken it. She only hoped Lucipor would not be there to witness it. She didn't think she could bear that.

Silvipor stood in the outer corridor beyond the room's portal. "What is your command, Master?" he asked, and his question felt like a betrayal to Petra. She reminded herself he was not truly one of them and turned her face away, wiping the seeping blood from her mouth, her jaw aching fiercely from the master's hand.

"Fetch me a rope. I am not to be disturbed otherwise."

"Yes, Master." Silvipor strode away without a glance in her direction. It surprised her Clarius's most loyal slave never suspected what she would do, but then he didn't know of her mother's poison.

19

With a strange sort of detachment, Petra realized the master had some sort of torture or hanging in mind. She felt herself floating outside of her body, wholly separate from her physical form, as if she were entering one of her own vivid memories. Was this a kind of self-protection? Was her ability to see images that weren't there going to save her from the pain—from death? What would it feel like to die? She determined not to cry out, no matter what the master inflicted upon her. He would not conquer her. She had already destroyed his lineage, his family. As he had destroyed hers. She did not regret it. And if she could figure out a way, she would kill him too.

"Come, murderess. Your death awaits." Clarius's voice, laced with certainty, made her anger boil over. She would not make this easy for him.

Petra struggled against him now, straining to wrest his fingers from her wrist. He stopped and backhanded her. Stunned and seeing strange lights within her vision, she shook her head, trying to keep her wits about her as more blood poured from her mouth. The master dragged her through the rest of the house and out into the deserted courtyard beyond. They crossed over the mosaics of the goddesses, and Petra cried out to them silently, begging them for mercy. For herself. For her father, a slave these many years in Rome. For Lucipor.

It was then that Petra glimpsed Lucipor in the flesh. He was running across the courtyard, carrying an unwieldy scythe in his hands. His face… *Oh, goddess*, his face. He meant to murder Clarius. She shook her head vehemently at him and stopped her struggle, letting the master yank her along. Yet Lucipor did not heed her. He had the same murderous look in his eyes that fueled Clarius.

Petra knew he, too, would soon be dead. And it would all be for nothing. What was she, anyway? Merely a summer dalliance for a slave as handsome as Lucipor. He could have gone on to fall truly in love, to marry another, worthier slave. Maybe they would even have been freed for good service and went on to live long lives among their children and grandchildren. But now, on this night, he was going to give his life foolishly in defense of hers, and she had no way to stop him.

Petra barely noticed when Silvipor handed a rough cord of rope to Clarius. She stared at the rope, feeling a grey despair filling her chest and limbs.

"Leave us," she heard the master say, finally noticing he was leading her into the men's bathhouse on the opposite side of the villa's courtyard. Secluded and deserted at this time of day, her screams would echo easily against the stones, which would please him greatly, she thought with dispassionate reasoning.

Being a woman and a slave, she had never been allowed in the baths, so she was strangely curious what it looked like. Torches burned against the gloom of the darkened circular room. It felt cavernous and at the same time the humid air encroached upon her, making her breathing quicken.

She realized this would be the last place she would ever see, and she regretted she had not shouted to Lucipor to stay away when she still had the chance. The other slaves—perhaps Silvipor—would have killed him by now. That thought reminded her to struggle, and her fantasies had her striking Clarius dead and racing out to rescue Lucipor. But it was just the madness that had overtaken them all. She tried to pull away from Clarius once more, but he was far too strong. His muscles bulged, he stood a head and a half taller, and his anger gave him a strength she could never hope to overcome.

He dragged her into the warm pool, until the water came up to her knees. She stumbled a bit, feeling confused at the comfort of the warm water surrounding her, the beauty of the torches, and the strange lights thrown up against the stones from the reflection of the pool. Beauty and comfort at a moment such as this? Was this a gift to her from the goddess or some new torture?

The master worked with quick precision, pulling her arms back around one of the columns surrounding the pool. When he circled back, he leered at her, his face too close for her to see anything but the hot anger in his eyes.

"Your blood will soon fill this pool, girl, and I will bathe in your death."

Petra didn't think. She kicked him as hard as she could. He let out a laugh, until they both heard shouts at the door of the bathhouse. With a sinking heart, she heard the distinctive sound of Lucipor's voice. For a moment, it brought her joy. It meant he was alive, but she knew it could not be for long. He was merely a boy, and these were men he would be fighting against.

The master ignored the shouts as he reached into the pouch at her waist. She realized she had completely forgotten the mortanine. He pulled the phial out and flashed it before her eyes.

"How would you like to die, girl? A slice to the throat in honor of your mother? Or would you prefer to honor my dead wife and child with a bit of poison to help you on your way?" He laughed again and unstoppered the phial, its clear, deadly poison sloshing within.

"You drink it, Master," she said, proud her voice was so steady and passionless, despite the blood she swallowed from the tear in her lip. "Your wife awaits you. I will even pay *Charon*'s toll for when you cross the *Acheron* to Hades."

This set him off. Clarius grabbed her by the hair and roughly pulled her head back. To her own disgust, she cried out from the pain. "No. You will drink and drink and drink until I hear your dying breath." He raised the phial up to her closed mouth and held her nose to force her mouth open.

"Let her go, Master."

Petra twisted her face around to see Lucipor. He held the tip of the scythe to the master's neck. Petra wanted to tell him with her eyes to leave them. She was dead anyway, but he had a chance to escape. Yet he would not look at her.

"You are a fool, boy. You wish to die too? I will hasten you to your end. But first you will watch."

"Release her, or I will kill you."

"The girl's breath is running out, boy." The master held the poison up to her lips. He was right. Her lungs seized as she strained against the ropes, trying in vain to break free.

Look at me, Lucipor, she wanted to scream. *Run as far away as you can. You cannot save me.*

Still his eyes watched Clarius's every move.

Petra shook violently, holding onto the last of her air, and then it all happened at once. Her mouth burst open, and Clarius tipped the phial into her mouth as Lucipor sliced a gaping hole across his master's throat. And so Petra's end began.

III

The First Death

July 13, 2 BC

PETRA SPIT THE POISON OUT INTO THE MASTER'S FACE AS HE DROPPED THE phial into the pool and released her to clutch at his throat. She was pleased, at least, to see much of the mortanine and blood from her lip had entered his mouth. But not all. She had ingested most of it, and now she felt the poison begin its deadly work.

Amid Lucipor's shouts and the clatter of the scythe on the stones, she felt a strange tingling spread out from her jaw and move quickly into her limbs. She felt her chest heave and her breathing come hard. Weakness washed over her, and she slumped against the ropes holding her against the column as Lucipor jumped into the pool beside her.

"Gods above, Petra. Let me take the poison from you." He held her head in his hands as he had done when he spoke of love to her not an hour ago. How things had changed since then…

"No, the poison will kill you too." With every word, she found it harder and harder to speak as a painful numbness spreading throughout her jawline and limbs turned into stabbing pains. "I murdered that poor woman and her baby, Lucipor. Let me die as I deserve."

Lucipor seemed not to hear her. He glanced over at Clarius, who had fallen back against the stone steps of the pool, his neck gaping wide and gushing blood down into the pool. "Clarius is dead. You, at least, have that comforting thought to carry you into death."

"Go now," she pleaded, hiding her eyes from Clarius's hideous body.

"Live for me."

"There is no life in me without you."

"I need you to live on, Lucipor. This was my choice. My revenge. You should have stayed away."

She wanted to push him from her, but her arms were restrained, and she felt them weakening as the moments passed. It wouldn't be long now. She didn't know if she was afraid to die. Everything was happening so fast. The pain was forcing all coherent thought from her mind.

Tears filled his eyes and he shook his head. "I cannot bear this." Lucipor forced her mouth to his and began to drink the blood and poison from her mouth. When he pulled back from her, she saw defeat in his eyes. He knew as well as she that he was too late. He pressed one hand to her heart and his other braced her back as her body shook uncontrollably against the column. They locked eyes, then, and no words came between them. His now-bloodied mouth touched hers again but this time it was a gentle kiss salted with his tears.

"I feel a strangeness in my jaws and arms. I will release you from your bonds while I have the strength."

In the corner, she saw a familiar form. "I see my mother now, over in the corner where the shadows are deep," Petra whispered, as her racing heart began to slow. "She is smiling."

"She awaits you. We will go together to meet her in the afterlife." He strode back through the water after he had released her, and she fell into his arms. They clung to each other as the death throes took them. Her other senses took over as she held to him. The smell of the torch smoke. The warmth of the water as it swirled gently between them. The musk of Lucipor's fear as it came in waves off his body. When her vision clouded, she whispered to him one last time.

"Come to me now and loosen me from blunt agony."

"Labor and fill my heart with fire," he answered in a breaking voice.

"Stand by me and be my ally—" Her arms lost all strength, and she fell against him.

"Always." Lucipor spoke no more as his forehead touched hers.

The last thing Petra saw was her mother's face in a flash of white light, and then the world faded into a final darkness.

Strange lights permeated the darkness of Petra's vision. She felt as though she were wrapped in a warm blanket. All was quiet, save for the sound of water rushing somewhere nearby. The river Acheron? But she had no payment for the boatman.

Petra lowered her arm and felt the swirl of water against her tingling skin. She felt arms surrounding her, and the closeness of an unmoving body clinging to hers.

Lucipor! Her eyelids flew open, and she realized she was still in the pool clinging to him. The torches burned low, and they were alone. No, not alone. The master lay unmoving against the steps as before, his blood sticking to the stones and dispersed through the water.

How could this be? How could she be alive? She had consumed the poison. She had felt her life passing into nothingness. Had the goddess answered her cries for mercy and raised her from the dead? And what of Lucipor?

She gently pulled away from him and examined his face. His head lolled against his neck and his body was pliable. Was the water keeping him warm and giving color to his skin?

She kissed his cheek and shook him with the gentlest of touches. "Wake, my love. Wake with me, and we will escape this madness." But he floated motionless in the pool, so she pulled him along toward the edge, dangerously near to Clarius.

The master was clearly dead. His skin had a sickly pallor, and his face lay frozen in the horror of his moment of death. Petra turned away in disgust, attempting in vain to pull him free of the water.

"Lucipor, please wake. Don't leave me here." Petra glanced around at the gloom. She thought it strange no slaves had come in. Then she remembered the master had commanded Silvipor not to disturb him. She realized Lucipor must have killed the servants guarding the door and dragged them inside the bathhouse to ensure no one would see their bodies. The light must be fading fast outside for him to have done that without being seen.

She shook her head as she pulled the wet strands of hair from his face. What madness it had been for him to try to save her. Yet somehow, he had, against all reason or explanation. She lived, and now she wondered if she could breathe life back into Lucipor.

A clatter right behind her made her jump to her feet. She held her hands up to defend herself but there was no one there. She risked a glance at the master again and discovered the dagger secured to his belt had shifted in the rippling water.

If Clarius somehow awoke as she did, he would come after them both. Of that she was certain. Petra stared at the dagger and thought about all the ways she could ensure he would not wake from the dead. The images flashed in a succession through her mind, and this alone made her heart beat faster and her hands sweat. She had already killed his wife and son. What was one more body to cross the river Acheron?

With careful hands, Petra slowly lifted the dagger from its elaborate sheath, her eyes ever on the master's face. Only the water moved his body. His eyes remained unchanged as they gaped up at the stone ceiling. Petra knelt at his side and held the dagger over his heart. She had seen a slave owner kill one of his slaves this way. It was in the market, in front of the entire crowd. The slave screamed for mercy, but no one in the open-mouthed throng moved to her defense. That was the day last winter when Petra had accompanied her mother to fetch herbs for a sick woman at the villa. The owner stabbed the woman in the heart over and over, and her screams echoed across the stones of the street and through the market-place. Most watched in fascination. Petra had looked away in horror, but not before she saw blood pour from the woman's chest, spraying across the man's already red face.

Would the master's blood mark her face too? Would he awaken in a rage? She had to do it. She had to be sure. She raised the dagger higher, turning her face away at the last moment so as not to have the vision of his second death as etched into her mind as the first.

"Petra."

The dagger clattered to the stones, and without thinking, Petra spun around to the lower steps to witness Lucipor's heavy-lidded eyes peering at her as if he did not know her. And yet he had said her name.

"Lucipor. Thank the goddess, you're alive."

He ran a hand over his face, and looked about him. "How…? I felt you die in my arms." He reached up to her, then, and she bent to kiss him and touch his face. He froze and pulled away.

"The master—?"

"He is dead. I thought we were too." She pointed at Clarius and was relieved to see he had not moved.

"How?"

"I don't know. I've seen this poison kill all manner of vermin. It killed the master's wife and child too."

"It makes no matter," he said, as he swiftly sat up and pulled her into an embrace. "You're alive. Nothing else in the world matters to me now."

"We won't last long if we don't flee the villa."

"We will make for Rome," he whispered.

"How will we make it past the slaves and servants loyal to the master?"

"Leave it to me. Where did you get that dagger?"

"I took it from him."

Lucipor picked it up and bade her to silence as he listened to the noises beyond the bathhouse.

"It is quiet out there. Dusk has fallen, if not night itself. Stay close behind me. We will keep to the shadows and run toward the fields."

"And from there the old road toward Rome?" she asked. The master's villa was far out into the fields and forests, far removed from the nearest village of Tibur on the outskirts of Rome. They had a long way to go.

He nodded as he got to his feet.

"Wait." She waded into the pool, hooked her bare toe around the chain holding the empty bottle of mortanine, and put it back into her sodden pouch. As she made her way back toward him, she caught his attention. "You remember the island in the master's lake?"

"Where Decimus's boy drowned last year."

"Yes, we must pass by there."

"The lake is out of our way. We need to put as much space between here and—"

"It's for our safety. Trust me."

Lucipor glanced down at the master. He hesitated for only a moment, and then shook his head. "We need to go before suspicion at the master's absence makes the house slaves come to investigate."

He took up her hand and pulled her away from Clarius's body, and they made their way silently on bare feet across the mosaic floor leading out of the bathhouse. Near the entrance, Petra gasped at the bodies of the master's most loyal slaves, Silvipor and Otho.

"Are they dead?"

"Only unconscious, I think. I caught them unawares but I didn't deliver killing blows," he replied, avoiding looking at them.

Petra held back as Lucipor scouted outside the door.

"There are two slaves loyal to the master at the far end of the courtyard and another two across from the entrance. Those two men are Eryx and Tros."

"Do you think they would let us pass? They are not known to favor Clarius."

"I think we should assume not, but they are not looking toward the bathhouse entrance, so we may be able to slip by them and hide behind the donkey cart."

He took hold of her hand and led her out into the shadows. Petra felt naked, exposed. Her tunic grew cold as the brisk night air touched its damp edges. A shiver of fear shook her as they crouched behind the horse cart. Dawn was approaching and the night was still mired in profound darkness.

"Now where?" Petra asked.

Lucipor glanced toward every corner of the courtyard, looking for their escape route.

"Stay away from the torch lights. They will expose you. We will run straight across and into the vineyard. If we get separated, meet by the old olive tree where we had our first kiss."

At first she thought him mad to suggest they run through the open courtyard, but then she realized the torches edging it were even less safe.

"Don't let go of my hand," she whispered, her heart hammering against her chest.

"Never, my love." He kissed her forehead, pulled her to her feet, and they were off running as silently and swiftly as they dared.

Shouts immediately resounded around them, but Petra couldn't gauge their origin. She did not stop, only focused on keeping up with Lucipor, whose strength and speed exceeded her own. She was amazed to discover that despite her death and resurrection, she could run faster than she ever had in her life. She was surprised she suffered no ill effects from the poison. She had all her faculties and her mind was clear.

"Faster, Petra. They are following."

She glanced back, then, and immediately wished she hadn't. Eryx and Tros were much too close. Lucipor dragged her deeper through the vineyard, and when they made it to the grove, darkness mercifully cloaked them. He halted their progress and bade her to crouch down behind an olive tree. They tried to steady their breathing as Tros passed close by, followed by Eryx who brandished a dagger similar to the master's thin blade.

"Do you see them?" Eryx called out.

"Silence, you fool," came Tros's reply as the men moved further into the grove.

In the weak light of a waning moon, Petra pointed south toward the lake. Lucipor nodded, steering them toward the open darkness of the furthest fields on the master's land. They continued for more than a mile in silence, until the fields turned into a forest and the ink-black lake lay directly ahead.

When he finally spoke, it startled her. "Why have we come here?"

"For the poison."

He stepped back from her, and even in the low light she saw the shock written in his eyes. "Why?"

"I told you. For our protection. If they try to search for us, we may be able to use it as a weapon."

"Knives and spears are better," he said, clearly frustrated at the lost time.

"There is another reason. I want to understand the mortanine flower's properties better. It both killed us and raised us from the dead. It must be the flower of the gods. We have to learn more."

He shook his head but did not protest further. "Tell me where it is and I will fetch it."

"On the island. The flower is a blood red, though you will not see that in the dark. It's a large flower and its leaves are tightly coiled and rising out around the center of each bloom like springs. We need the flower itself, I think, but bring the whole plant just in case. Gather three of them, but do not let the leaves or petals touch your mouth."

As Lucipor hurriedly stripped off his tunic and swam out to the island, Petra listened to the wind in the trees and the frogs talking among the reeds along the bank. If the day hadn't been filled with such horrors, she might have found this moment peaceful.

"Petra?" he called out.

"Did you find the flowers?"

"Yes, I have them." He came out of the water, shivering.

"Thank you," she whispered, pulling him into an embrace, his wet skin dampening her nearly dry clothing. It felt strange to her, as if they hadn't just gone through death and resurrection together.

He pulled away to dress and began to tell her of his plan. "We will travel by night and sleep during the day. It will keep us warmer and help us move unseen along the roads and paths."

"I will follow your lead."

He glanced up at her and gave her a reassuring smile.

She stopped him before he made his way down the path leading away from the lake and toward Rome far to the southwest.

"Lucipor——" she hesitated, biting her lip.

"Yes?"

"Do you think the master still lives?"

This time his smile was laced with sadness. "If he is, he will never stop hunting us."

IV

The Draw

"DO YOU FEEL IT TOO?" PETRA ASKED LUCIPOR AS THEY SETTLED CLOSE together by the fire he had built for them at dawn. They had walked all night and found a hiding place deep in a quiet wood. Petra felt no pain or exhaustion; she wasn't even chilled in the cool morning air. This seemed strange given what they had been through.

He glanced up sharply, as if he knew exactly what she meant. Then he looked away, toward the new dawn. "I feel a ravenous hunger even as I have no desire for food."

"What do you hunger for?" She was almost afraid to ask because she felt the same but had no words for it.

Lucipor opened his mouth to speak but bit his lip and stoked the fire instead. She waited until he glanced up at her again out of the corner of his eye. He almost looked nervous. At the encouragement in her eyes, he finally spoke.

"I hunger for you. More than I ever have before. Before my desire was a pleasure. Now it is a pain I cannot control."

"I feel it too," she whispered, heat rising in her cheeks. "Do you think… it has something to do with the mortanine?"

"It must." He picked up one of the flowers by the stem and twirled it between his fingers. "I feel as strong and powerful as a god."

"You cannot say such things, Lucipor. The gods will strike you down."

"Don't you feel it too? As though nothing can harm you? I feel as if

31

I could take on ten men and still be ready for more."

She touched his arm, feeling for the muscles to see if they had grown. He did feel stronger. She pulled back to study him. He seemed more beautiful than he had ever been somehow—this despite all their walking and lack of sleep. The brown of his eyes was clearer, the curls of his hair were kissed by the rising sun, and his skin seemed to glow from within. He had never been more beautiful to her, despite the dirt smudging his skin and tunic.

"The only man I want to kill is the master—"

Lucipor grasped her arm. "No, you must never call him that again. He is no longer our master. We are free."

"Then you are no longer Lucipor. I will call you by his father's name, Lucius, because now you are your own master."

He smiled and nodded.

Petra touched the slave collar at his neck. He touched it, too, remembering it yet remained, a testament to what they had been but were no longer. She frowned, wondering if she could remove it. She knelt and examined the welded bronze of the thin band. She grabbed hold and yanked as hard as she could. The metal cracked in half, the collar slipping from his chafed and raw neck. He glanced back at her, shock widening his eyes as his fingers curled over the symbol of his imprisonment.

"How did you do it?" he asked.

"I'm strong now, Lucius," she said, loving the sound of his new name on her lips. "You help me." When he wrested the collar from her, she let it drop without another thought.

He reached out to her, his shaking fingers touching her cheek.

"How is it you are still so fair? You have gone through death and back, and yet you look as if you have slept for days."

"You have the look of a god about you too," she whispered.

"I am alive and free because of you, Petra. I owe you everything I am or will ever be."

When his lips touched hers, the madness of desire she had felt growing inside of her since they left the villa burst open, as if she were hurtling into the center of the sun, which even now warmed her face as it shifted through the trees.

"I need you." He held both sides of her face with trembling fingers. "Can you—will you have me?"

"I—yes," she whispered, her breath quickening. Every touch was like being burned by a cold fire. It pained her to the point of agony, and yet she craved more. "I feel like I am losing control of my wits."

"I already have." He stripped off his tunic and pulled her against his chest. The heat of the fire next to them was warm, but Lucius's body was as hot as a fever. His kiss deepened and her heart pounded with the ecstasy coursing through her in waves. Her body clung to his instinctively, until they knelt together, locked in a tight embrace. He held her back and she clung to his shoulders. This was no mere kiss. There was an otherworldly power moving between them, a power she could not control.

"It's too much," she said, but her mouth drew down for more. The madness driving her had taken over. She screamed but she could not stop.

"Petra! Petra, you must let me go... You must—"

Something moved in the air between them... Something pulled at her. No, she was pulling him into her. Petra knew she had to stop. Had to let him go. But she could not. She needed him more than she had ever needed anything in her whole life.

All at once, she felt the power of his body, the grace of his mind, and the surrender of his life as she drew deeply from his essence. She did not even have to kiss him now. A tendril of vapor moved through the air between their mouths.

"Petra..." His fear succumbed to his desire, and then she knew he felt it, too, felt the rapture consuming her. But he was weakening, his arms releasing her now, his consciousness slipping away. She gently lay him down among the leaves and shook his head to rouse him, pressed her fingertips to his temples. She felt the inescapable power, the undeniable draw. As Lucius's beautiful eyes began to close, his mind opened up to her. And then Petra was there inside him, looking out through his eyes.

Lucipor walked a dusty road. He held the hand of a man, and when he looked up, he saw his father's blood-smeared face, watched as the irons at his wrist chafed his skin raw.

"Where are we going, pater?"

"To our new master."

"Will he be better than the last?"

"It does not matter. You must do as he says."

"We go to his villa now?" Lucipor asked, tripping over a rock and landing hard in the dust of the road.

"Yes, we journey to Villa di Avidus today."

His father stopped to pick him up, and the young man who led the caravan, the one who had bound Lucipor's father's chains to the back of his horse's saddle, shouted back at him.

"I told you to keep up, old man. Now your son will never forget what it means to obey." He slapped the horse's rump, and the horse took off at a swift gallop, dragging Lucius's father with him through the dust and rock.

Lucius screamed until his voice grew hoarse, until his body could produce no more tears. When the slaves and their guards finally caught up to the young man on the horse, Lucipor no longer saw his father. He saw only the trail of blood that remained.

"Let this be a lesson to you, boy," the young man shouted as he dismounted at the gates of Villa di Avidus. "I am Clarius. One day, I will be your master. See that you do not disappoint me as your father has."

When the memory faded into the morning's harsh light, Petra felt Lucius's body fall to the leaves, his eyes lifeless.

"No, Lucius…" Her desire to consume him turned to ash in her mouth. She collapsed over his prone body, dissolving into wracking sobs. "Come back," Petra whispered into his lips as the vapor vanished into the harsh morning light.

She did this. She killed him with her own power. Just as she had orchestrated the deaths of Clarius's wife and newborn. It didn't matter that she had tried to stop Clarius from giving Constantia the poison. It didn't matter that she had no idea she had the power to kill with a kiss. She was no different than Clarius. She was the one who deserved to die. Not Lucius. Never Lucius.

Clarius was right all along. She was a murderess.

V

The Grove

"L ucius... Lucius? Please wake up!" Petra felt his chest for breaths but there was nothing. Tears blinded her as she shook his shoulders gently. "Come back to me," she whispered.

But he lay unmoving in the leaves and moss beneath the trees. Quelling her rising fear, Petra thought back to the bathhouse, to Clarius. She wondered again how they had survived the mortanine, a poison she had seen kill vermin within minutes. Perhaps they needed to drink more poison for the full effects. Yet how did she kill Lucius, then? Was it the strange vapor she had pulled from his body? Tears pricked her eyes as she looked down at his peaceful face. They had been kissing, and then she saw his memories inside her head, something she had never been able to do before.

She instinctively touched her lip where Clarius's hand had drawn blood. Could that be it? Both the master and Lucius had swallowed her blood along with the poison. She knew nothing of science or philosophy or healing, but she knew beyond any doubt she and Lucius were no longer the same as they had been. To her, it seemed, the key was in her blood. She thought about letting him drink from her but dismissed it. Though, she knew it could not harm him now, given that he survived it before. The idea seemed foolish, even prideful, to believe her blood had such restorative effects. Perhaps they had not ingested enough poison to fully kill them. But it didn't explain what she had done to Lucius just now.

35

Petra let out a cry of rage and frustration. "Wake up!"

Still, he did not move. She glanced around the wood, as the day grew hotter with the rising sun. Then she heard faint voices in the distance. People were walking through the forest. Travelers? Or Clarius's servants? Did they hear her cry out and come to investigate? She fought back tears as she looked at Lucius, at his body so exposed, so vulnerable.

The people continued to approach. She heard men's voices. It had to be a search party from the villa. A tremor moved up her spine. The only idea she had left was to give Lucius her blood in the vain hope it would revive him. She had no water to douse the fire, and evidence they had been here was everywhere. There was no time to help Lucius and hide all traces they had been here before the men caught up with them.

She took up the dagger, bit her lip hard, and sliced through her wrist. The pain burned. She tried not to cry out, biting her lip harder and harder. She let her tears fall unchecked as she held open his mouth.

"I'm going to try to save you, Lucius," she whispered. "This blood is the only thing I have left to give."

Her blood dripped into his mouth, and she pressed her wrist to his lips. She didn't know how much to give, but she let her wrist rest gently against him while she listened to the voices draw closer.

"There! I see the smoke again, in the middle of that grove of trees." She heard the familiar shout of Eryx and her heart fell.

She couldn't move Lucius without alerting the men to their presence. She began to see flashes of their tunics and heard the crackle of the leaves underfoot as they quickened their pace through the trees.

"I dare not stay any longer," she whispered, wrapping her wrist in a strip of cloth she ripped from her tunic. "I won't go far, and I won't leave you until you come back to me." She kissed him, tasting the metallic sweetness of her blood on his lips, and whispered, "I love you," before she slipped away.

Taking care to slip quietly over the moss and avoid the leaves, Petra moved behind a massive overturned tree trunk, its twisted roots hiding her body.

"They are near. I can smell their blood. I can almost taste it." When Clarius's voice rang out, and he stepped through the trees into the clearing, Petra gasped. He stood, alive and strong, a grey pallor to his skin and a bandage wrapped around his neck above his tunic the only evidence there had been a life-and-death struggle between them.

"Look, the boy is there by the fire!" Tros shouted.

"He's mine. Find the girl."

Petra watched Clarius, hoping he would believe Lucius had died and leave his body alone.

"Master, he's dead," Eryx said.

Clarius's expression, at first triumphant at finding his prey, flashed to anger. Anger that his chance to kill Lucius had been thwarted?

"*Vae!*" Clarius shouted, glancing wildly around at the remnants of their makeshift camp. He kicked Lucius hard in the stomach, and his body heaved up in response, but he did not wake. Petra rose to go out to him, but she didn't know how to help. She already knew Clarius's strength far exceeded her own. She had no chance at all against the three of them. And if somehow Lucius did awaken, he would need her later.

"He was my kill. Mine!" Clarius shouted a string of obscenities and kicked over a smoldering branch at the edge of the fire, scattering ash over Lucius's bare chest and the mortanine flowers beside him. "How was it done?" he shouted at his men. "The poison?"

"He has blood dripping from his mouth, Master. The poison must have finally killed him." Eryx had taken a step back, fearful he would be an unwitting recipient of Clarius's rage.

"The girl must have died, too, Master," Tros offered.

Eryx nodded, studying Lucipor. "The boy likely left her behind somewhere."

"We would have found her, you fool. No, she left him after he died and continued on." Clarius glanced out toward the main road further down into the valley below. "I am certain they were headed toward Rome."

"He might have buried her or hid her body," Tros offered with a hesitant voice.

"No. I can smell her blood. She's still alive, but she won't be for long. I swear it. And before I kill her, the first thing she is going to tell me is how we cheated death."

Petra listened to this in silence. Inside she was screaming. Her palms were sweating, and her face flushed hot. Clarius somehow thought she knew what had caused their astounding recovery. As if she would ever truly know.

"Master, what do you instruct?"

Clarius narrowed his eyes and knelt in front of the last remaining remnants of the fire. "I told you to track her. As for this slave, if I cannot kill him, I will burn him."

Petra almost cried out but covered her mouth instead. She looked for anything she could use to distract Clarius. A rock protruded from the soil at her feet. Too small to make much noise, but she hoped it would make them assume she might be hiding in the opposite direction. Leaning back, she threw the rock as hard as she could toward the northeast. It slammed against a massive boulder that overhung a ravine, immediately drawing the attention of all three men.

The master waved them toward the ravine and fell into step behind them. Petra leaned against the tree trunk and tried to steady her breathing. She did not move until they were well away from the campsite. She hurried to Lucius's side and noticed his abdomen had already started to form the beginnings of an ugly bruise. She touched it but jumped back when she felt movement under her fingers.

"You're alive!" She could see it now; his chest moved in and out, his breathing labored but steady.

Lucius's head lolled but he slowly opened his eyes.

"Petra?" He seemed confused, unaware of his surroundings. He blinked several times, squinting into the sunlight behind her.

"I will explain everything when we are safe. Are you well enough to walk?"

"I'm not sure," he said too loudly.

"Keep your voice down. Clarius is near."

"How?"

She heard movement through the forest again.

"Let me help you up. He is coming back." Petra pulled him to a standing position. She picked up the mortanine flowers, ripped their petals off, and stuffed them into a hidden pocket in her tunic.

"My side hurts," he whispered when he raised his arms to slip into his scratchy woolen tunic.

"I know. Clarius kicked you when you were… when you died." He stared at her as he let her lead him over to her hiding place behind the overturned tree.

"I died? What happened to me? I remember I was—"

She put a finger to his lips. Whether she stopped him for safety's sake or because she was afraid he would remember the truth of what she had done to him, she didn't know.

Clarius and his men crashed into the clearing where their fire lay scattered.

When Lucius caught a glimpse of Clarius in between the roots, he sobered instantly. So great was Clarius's rage, only unintelligible gibberish came out of his mouth as he rampaged around the camp kicking trees and scattering leaves over the dying fire.

His voice calm, his eyes focused, Lucius turned to her. "We have to run for it. Can you do it?"

"Yes." She touched his stomach. "Can you?"

"I'll make it. You go first. Quiet at the beginning—watch your step—

and then when I say, you need to run like the wind. Head away from Rome, deep into the forest. We need to get lost, so they will find it difficult to follow."

They took off as quietly as they were able toward a dark grove of pines to the northwest, away from the Tibur River and the old road to Rome. When Lucius pressed her to run, they heard Clarius's deafening scream in the distance, his voice echoing through the trees like the voice of a god.

"When I find you, coward, you will beg me for death. I will make your life an endless torment. By the gods, I swear it!"

They were many miles away when Petra and Lucius finally slowed their pace. Sweat poured from their bodies in the full heat of the afternoon, despite the dappled shade of the forest canopy overhead. When her breathing slowed enough for her to talk, Petra beckoned him over to a fallen tree trunk. He followed, wiping moisture from his forehead.

"You asked me what happened, Lucius, and it is only fair I tell you the absolute truth."

"I remember bits and pieces," he said, wariness in his tone.

"You died because of me."

"What do you mean? How? You could never overpower me."

"But I did. We kissed, and then a vapor moved between us. I could see it in the air between our mouths. It moved from you into me. It gave me strength—your strength. It made my desire for you unquenchable. I could not stop. I wanted more and more, even though you begged me to stop. And then…"

He remained silent for several moments, as he looked away toward the sun beating through the oaks and pines. Finally, he simply said, "And then?"

"You died in my arms." She was the one who looked away this time, down to her clasped fingers as she squeezed them together so hard they turned white.

"I don't understand. Such a thing is not possible."

"Remember we once thought cheating death was impossible. What of us now? Are we not living proof of the impossible?"

"Yes, but—"

"Whatever it was, it took your life completely. I pulled the essence from your body and stole your strength as a thief steals a loaf of bread from the market."

"How did you do it?"

She frowned, confused. "I told you. I—"

"No, how did you bring me back?"

"I—I am not sure."

"Petra," he said, studying her face intensely, "you forget how well I know you. There's something you're not telling me."

"I fed you my blood."

His eyebrows rose so high they reached the dark hair falling across his forehead. He touched his mouth absently where her blood still stained his lower lip.

"I don't know if it was that which saved you, or if it was merely time."

He thought long about her words, rising from the tree trunk to pace about.

"Lucius?" she finally said.

"Hmm…?" He barely registered her voice so lost was he in his thoughts.

"Can you forgive me?"

At that, he glanced up sharply, his thoughts immediately forgotten. He walked back and sat beside her, grasping her hand in his.

"Always."

Her gaze rose to meet his, and she saw he meant it.

"You had no way of knowing this would happen. Something has changed both of us. We are no longer human. We are beyond human."

"No, that's—"

"Impossible? You were right when you said we were living proof of the impossible. Think about it. Even though we must have run nearly twenty miles last night, you don't feel hungry or thirsty, do you?"

She shook her head.

"All three of us escaped poisoning and death to live again." Lucius touched her temple with his fingers. "And you pulled the life from my body with a simple kiss."

Petra felt almost dizzy with the implications. What would it mean for them now? Would they always be in hiding? Would Clarius Avidus track them to the ends of the world looking for answers?

"What should we do?" she asked.

"I think we should learn all we can about what happened to us."

"I agree."

40

"And we need to learn to defend ourselves. Clarius will find us again. When he does, we must be ready."

"How will we survive him?"

He offered up a half-smile. "You can give him your kiss of death."

"Please don't tease. I—"

Lucius ran a finger over her lips to silence her. "I don't know why, but just the thought of it makes me want to kiss you again."

The Prima Sanguis

Sicily

February 21, 1723

THE LADY TURNED FROM AURELIA AND TOUCHED LUCIUS'S HAND. "DO YOU remember all those months we wandered Rome looking for my father?"

Lucius's smile was wistful. "I only wish we had found him."

"You never received word of him, Madame?" Aurelia asked.

Petra shook her head. "The last time I was in Rome, the slave drivers had marched my family into the slave market and sold us to the highest bidder. I thought myself lucky to be sold to Master Lucius Avidus at the time. He was considered a kind and fair master."

"He was, but he was a slave master all the same," Lucius said.

Petra nodded. "Little did we know what horrors would come of it. My father had been sold to a wealthy patrician in Rome, but beyond that, I knew nothing. We searched in secret, always worried we'd turn a corner and run into Clarius or one of his servants. It was all in vain. We never found him."

"Eventually, we abandoned our search and headed south," Lucius said.

"What happened next? Did you stay in Italy?"

"For a time, in a tiny village that doesn't exist anymore," Petra answered. "It was there that we studied my blood. I made a new batch of mortanine, and we did experiments with it. At first with rodents—"

Aurelia couldn't help but laugh. "Ah, yes, the immortal rats. I remember the experiments you did in later centuries on those."

Lucius smiled. "Well, immortal until they desiccated into nothingness."

"I think you should have kept some alive. We'd have a fair number of pets by now, don't you think?"

Petra feigned shock and shook her head. "Over my dead body."

They all smiled at the irony in that pronouncement.

"You experimented on yourselves, surely?" Aurelia asked.

"Oh, yes. We knew after several weeks of testing that the mortanine was required for turning an immortal."

"And that Petra's blood was the true restorative to keep us young forever." Lucius thumbed Petra's cheek affectionately. "You're my own personal savior, milady."

"And you're mine," Petra said.

"Was it at this point you realized you no longer had need of food or drink to survive?"

Lucius nodded. "Of course, the desire for the taste of food and wine never goes away, does it?"

Aurelia smiled and shook her head. "You learned quite soon that sleep wasn't necessary either, I assume?"

"Yes. Really, we discovered that the first night in the grove, when we ran from Clarius."

"That may be true," Lucius said, "but I'll never tire of having this woman in my bed in the darkest hours of the night to while away the hours." He patted Petra's knee and grinned at her.

"I don't doubt it," Aurelia said with a laugh.

"For months and months we wandered this way," Petra said, "crisscrossing through Italy, always keeping to ourselves. Along the way, we acquired many things: valuable trinkets, fine clothing, money. But we never stopped worrying Clarius would find us. We knew it was inevitable. With an eternity of time looming ahead, how could any of us hide from each other forever?"

Lucius looked away, toward the window. "We also knew we had something Clarius needed more than anything else in the world, something he would stop at nothing to find again: Petra's blood."

VI

The Mortanine

Tivoli

August 13, 1 AD

"THIS IS MADNESS, PETRA."

Lucius continued to give her grief as they made their way toward the lake near Villa di Avidus where the mortanine flowers grew. Petra didn't want to argue any further. She just held up the empty poison phial hanging around her neck. She had long since kept it dangling between her breasts, always at the ready to use against Clarius.

"All you heard were rumors," Petra said. "And we must have more. You know we will have need of it if he comes for us."

"I disagree. It obviously didn't kill any of us. The last thing we want is for him to discover its power and people the world with killers like him."

"Like us, you mean."

Lucius glanced sideways at her. "You didn't hear the villagers talking. You didn't see the fear in their eyes."

"But none of them had actually been to the villa."

"They knew those who had. They said he never leaves... that he looks like a monster now."

She shook her head, not wanting to believe it. "We only need a small bunch of flowers, and then we can be on our way. He won't even know we're here."

Lucius frowned at her but pressed on down the dusty path through the forested lands leading toward the lake.

"I doubt Clarius still lives at the villa," Petra said, mostly to distract him from his annoyance.

"I wouldn't think he'd leave his family's ancestral lands and all the power and wealth that comes with it. He also likely thinks we haven't gone far."

"Maybe he's dead," she mused.

"Why would he be? We're still alive. As far as we know, nothing can kill any of us now."

"He hasn't ingested my blood in nearly a year. We've already seen this with the rats. After three months they began to desiccate. And you…"

Lucius frowned. She didn't say it, but they both remembered what had happened to him. After twelve months, the tips of his fingers had faded to grey and faint black lines had laced his skin. When she let him drink from her again, his youthful skin came back, and his agitation and anger dissipated.

"I almost want to find him, so we can see the effects of his blood withdrawal." *And then kill him*, she thought.

"No, don't even think it. You remember how dangerous he is. The risk is too great."

"But think of what we could learn. You'll finally know if you're stuck with me forever, or if you can leave me to explore the far reaches of the Earth on your own."

He immediately walked back and pulled her into a kiss that took her breath away.

"You're stuck with *me* forever, Petra, so it matters not."

While they had yet to attempt sex, they had long since learned how to kiss without taking each other's lives—though it was not without difficulty. It surprised them both how hard the desire was to control. They had to pull away when they started to feel the vapors coming. They began to call the phenomenon an Essentian draw because when the drawing began, it felt as though their life essences were being pulled out of their bodies.

"You may not always want me, Lucius. We have no idea what the future holds, or even how long we will or can live."

He kissed her again, long and full, his soft lips exploring her own gently. When he finally released her, he whispered into her ear, tickling the skin at her neck.

"As I said before, it matters not. I will never let you go."

She covered his lips with her fingers and pulled back from his tight embrace. "What will we do, Lucius, if we cannot die?"

He grinned. "Simple: we will live forever."

She frowned and playfully punched his arm. He continued on down the path with a smile on his face, pulling her by the hand. Glancing ahead, she glimpsed a small sliver of the lake between the trees.

"We made it."

"Good, let's hurry." He quickened their pace. "I suppose I am to be your errand boy once again?" He removed his sandals and wiggled his toes into the pebbles warmed by the sun at the lake's shore. A flock of goldfinches skirted the water's still surface as they came in for a landing amid the reeds.

Petra flashed him a grin. "No, this time I'm coming with you. It's an excellent day for a swim, don't you think?" She reached up and drew him into a kiss. For a moment, they both abandoned all time and reason, drawing down deeper into a connection they alone in the world could ever experience. It was Lucius who pulled away when he began to feel the draw.

"Let us finish this and be gone," he whispered. "We must not linger."

He stripped off his tunic while she only removed her sandals. Lucius held the bag they had brought to carry the flowers, and then they both sank with delight into the cool waters.

The last time Petra swam in the lake was when her mother asked her to fetch mortanine to combat a severe rat infestation they were having in the slave quarters at the villa one year.

She swam alongside Lucius who proceeded to playfully splash her. She dunked him under, and they both laughed. When they reached the little island, which took no more than an hour to walk across at its longest length, he pulled her from the water.

"I'm happy to see the flowers are actually in bloom this year," she said, wringing out her tunic and taking a look around at the patches of mortanine flowers scattered among the shrubs, grass, and occasional tree. She had always loved coming here to the lake. The island itself, though small, had always looked like a place she would want to live on forever.

"Why wouldn't they be in bloom?" Lucius asked, bending down to study a cluster of them at his feet. The mortanine flowers had a similar shape to full red roses, but their petals curled into a more shell-like, concave form. Each flower spread from a deep mahogany at its center to a blood red at the petal tips, which Petra found appropriate given the flower's properties. In bright contrast, yellow-green leaves wound around each flower in tiny, tight spirals. She had never seen mortanine growing anywhere else.

"Some years, the conditions aren't right for them to bloom." She lifted her wet tunic to remove the dagger strapped to her thigh. "I remember my mother coming back from the lake the year of the awful drought complaining she had lost another year's batch."

"How did your mother even know about mortanine's uses? Did she know what it could do to humans? To us?"

"Much of midwifery is reducing a pregnant woman's pain. Herbs are most often used for that purpose, so my mother was quite skilled in the use of herbs and such things. If she ever learned it could change humans in such strange ways, she never told me. She only used it to kill vermin around the villa as far as I know."

"I suppose we have your mother to thank for her skill and curiosity."

"Yes, though there is the matter of my blood that we still do not truly understand."

"Given that we can survive on your blood alone, I am content, for now at least, to rely on you." He glanced up at her, looking hopelessly shy and embarrassed, holding out a bunch of the deadly red flowers in his hand to her in offering. "You who set my heart on fire." The desire in his eyes made her long for a time when Clarius was no more, when they could make love under a morning sun surrounded by the lake and the mortanine flowers and not fear for the future.

"I'm the one on fire, Lucius." With a smile, Petra rested her palm over his heart and stole another kiss as they crushed the blooms between them.

Eventually, they had gathered enough flowers to make several batches of mortanine poison, so they secured their bags and swam back across the lake.

As Petra squeezed water from her tunic and put on her sandals, she thought again about Clarius and all the rumors they had heard about him.

"Lucius," she began slowly, "the rumors about Clarius…"

"I know what you would say, Petra, but if you think we would survive an encounter with that bastard, you are wrong."

"I do think we would survive. Because we did the first time. And Clarius doesn't know how all this works."

"How could it possibly be worth the risk?"

"It isn't the risk to us I am worried about." It was partly her worry, but she wasn't about to share that with Lucius. "It is his risk to others. He has the same power we do. The same strength. The same desire to pull the life force of others from their bodies and kill them. If the rumors are to be believed, I do not doubt he has killed many people in the time we've been away, perhaps even some of our friends among the slaves. If what we have is true immortality, Lucius, think of all those he could murder until the end of time. Because we know what kind of man he is, those deaths will be on our heads too."

"What are you saying?"

She could tell by the tone of his voice he knew where this conversation was leading.

"I'm saying we have the advantage. Now. Today. We can catch him unaware and do away with him forever."

"And if he captures us? If he kills us?"

"If he does, I will wake you with my bloody kiss of life." She smiled, but it fell flat.

He laced his second sandal and began to chew on his lip, always an indicator he was seriously considering a proposition.

"If he has stationed guards, I don't see how we can infiltrate the villa's walls," he countered.

"Let's just get there, and then decide if there is a way to enter unseen."

"And if we find there is no way without great risk?"

"Then I promise we will take our flowers and go."

"I cannot lie." He frowned, and then wiped it from his face and looked at her long and hard. "I have wanted his death since…"

"Since your father's death."

He squinted at her. "How did you know that?"

Petra looked down, feeling rather ashamed she had seen his memory and never told him of it. "I saw it in your mind. On the day I killed you—"

Lucius pulled her into an embrace. "No, I have told you before. You were not to blame. Being that close to you before I—before it was over—was the single most pleasurable moment of my life."

"I saw only pain in your eyes."

"As you well know, an Essentian draw is both a pleasure and a pain. If I ever truly die, Petra, I want it to be in your arms."

"There's only one man I want to kill, Lucius, and that man will never be you."

VII

The Bargain

August 13, 1 AD

"CAN WE ENTER THROUGH THE SERVANTS' DOOR?" PETRA ASKED LUCIUS, hiding her bag of flowers in the shadows under a broken donkey cart. The walls surrounding the Villa di Avidus stood cold and uninviting today, but Petra remembered a time when Lucius Avidus still lived, when the villa felt like home. It never would again.

"I think so, but it is the heat of the day, and it's strange to hear no sounds or voices coming from the courtyard."

Petra nodded. "Not even the sounds of the donkeys or pigs. Do you think Clarius is here?"

"It's possible. We need to be careful."

"Are you ready?" she asked, rising from her crouched position and pulling her dagger from its sheath.

"Wait, Petra." Lucius pulled her back down. "I want you to promise me something. If our plans go ill, and you have a chance to escape… take it. Do not try to save me."

"I am in far less danger than you are. You know this. I would rather die than abandon you, but we both know *that* is impossible. We will survive this day."

His deep frown told her he did not agree, but he made no further demands. She pulled away from him and made her way toward the door. It was slightly ajar. More and more she wondered if Clarius had quit the villa altogether. If he had, they could raid it for anything useful he left behind.

When Petra slipped into the outer courtyard, the stench hit her before the images registered in her mind. Bodies lay everywhere, strewn across the mosaics and stones and scattered hay of the courtyard, most left to rot in dried pools of blood fading into the tiled images of the gods below them. The horror of their deaths lay frozen in their decaying eyes, and their torn-out throats were laid open to the elements.

"What happened here?" she whispered. but she knew the answer before the words left her.

It was indiscriminate. Servants, slaves, and men and women and children in the more elaborate garb of plebeians and patricians lay dead before them. She even spotted several Roman soldiers among them.

Petra stepped out of the shadows of the wall surrounding the courtyard to examine a body more closely, but Lucius pulled her back. His face didn't show horror.

Anger moved from his eyes to curl his lips into a snarl. "Clarius murdered them all."

"He didn't just murder them. He drank from them. From their necks, like an animal. Is that how he gains strength? How he feeds?"

Petra saw a change come over him. His chest heaved, his hands curled into white-knuckled fists, his body trembled with a growing rage. She touched his arm, and he shook his head, as if to tell her it was not safe to come near him.

"We will find him and kill him," she said simply, shocked at her own lack of emotion. She felt nothing, but she was determined to see Clarius pay for his crimes. For her mother. For Lucius's father. For all the innocent victims who lay before them. She stepped again into the full light of the day and marched across the mosaics of the gods among the bodies of the dead.

Such was their anger that they no longer cared to hide their presence, entering the house through the master's entrance as they had always been forbidden to do as slaves. In the *lararium*, the shrine off to the side of the *atrium* pool, the altar had been destroyed, its elaborate stonework crushed into pieces and scattered across the damaged mosaic floor. Petra covered her nose as they inched past a bloated body whose legs half floated in the water, his blood turning the color of the water a hideous shade she could not even name.

"He has become a monster," she said.

"I am what you made me, slave."

The moment Petra heard Clarius's voice, she knew without seeing he had become something far beyond what they had. When she turned, she didn't immediately see him, but then a slight movement from the shadows along the far wall caught her attention. She thought him at first one of the bodies, and even as he moved, he looked as one dead. His skin had taken on a dark grey pallor, his eyes glowed a pale silver, and black veins wove across his jaw, neck, and forehead. She recoiled at the sight of him.

"You have gone mad, Clarius." Lucius strode forward, unafraid, and Petra knew his use of their old master's praenomen was purposeful.

"I am what I have always been."

"True. But no longer. You will not live out this day, Clarius Avidus. You will answer for your crimes."

"For the killing of my mother," Petra said, walking forward to stand beside Lucius.

"And the murder of my father."

"So my little slave children have returned to seek revenge, have they?" Clarius slowly rose to his feet, taking another swig of wine from the half-empty bottle in his hand as he did so.

"We seek justice for the wrongs done to us, and to every life you have taken here," he said, his voice unwavering.

Clarius laughed. "I am a god now. No man can touch me."

"You forget we were made in the same way," Petra reminded him.

"Yes, and we'll get to that before I drink you dry. I wonder how you'll taste compared to these humans, Petra. Sweeter? Or as sour as your soul?"

"Do not underestimate our strength," Lucius countered, his voice betraying no hint of fear.

Petra shared his confidence, even though they were surrounded by dozens of Clarius's kills. Her desire to see him fall far outweighed the chance of losing her own life.

Clarius scoffed. "I cannot die. You saw to that when you poisoned me. You are responsible for this." He waved his hand toward the bodies. "For all of them."

"You alone bear responsibility," she said.

"…And the power their blood gave me," he finished, shaking out his taut arm muscles which, despite their desiccated appearance, had grown in size and strength since she had last seen him.

Petra scoffed at that. "You look like you will crumble into the dust at any moment."

Clarius narrowed his eyes at her, the insult getting under that hideous grey skin of his. Then he dropped the wine bottle and began his old pacing ritual, the one that always signaled the slow-building rage that would soon turn into a storm.

"I searched for you for many long months," he finally said. "I listened for rumors, traveled to many countries. I would have found you eventually. Something in your blood calls to me, slave girl. I can almost taste you from here." Clarius seemed not to realize he was speaking aloud or that Lucius was still in the room. Her old master stared at her, his body inching toward her even as his hatred for her seemed to hold him back. She had never seen him stare at her with such lust. He had certainly taken his fill of other slave girls a little older than she was through the years. She had always been too young for his tastes, which was unusual for patrician men. Most preferred young boys or girls for their pleasure.

Clarius seemed to shake himself out of his trance when her own stare turned into a scowl.

He matched her expression, then, and when he spoke, it was a demand. "You will tell me how it was done."

"I owe you nothing," Petra said.

"Save death," Lucius added.

"Before this ends, I will extract from you the answers I seek. You will tell me what I want to know, and then you will beg me for death."

Petra took his threat seriously and thought about whether she should reveal what part her blood played in his immortality. She had no idea if it would put them in more danger or protect them from Clarius's wrath. She decided not to tell him, but stood at the ready, raising her dagger to Clarius.

"When you die today, *Master*," she said with pure disgust, "I will make certain you never come back."

Lucius rushed ahead, his dagger in hand and a shout of rage erupting from his chest as if he'd held it back for decades. Petra was on his heels as Clarius waited for them. At the last moment, Clarius reached for the dagger at his belt and threw it at him, lodging it deep into his left thigh. Lucius grunted in pain, as Clarius slipped aside with preternatural anticipation.

Petra attacked and Clarius laughed at her clumsy attempt to stab him in the heart. He deftly shifted on his feet to avoid her. Lucius continued his forward thrust and went for Clarius's abdomen. He blocked him with an elbow and stepped in to punch Lucius in the jaw. Before he could recover, Petra jumped on Clarius's back and attempted to slice open his neck, but he threw her off. She fell on top of a foul-smelling body propped against the wall. She quickly scrambled off, holding back the urge to vomit.

Clarius spun away and ran off toward the back of the house and down the stairs where the servants' rooms and kitchen were located. Lucius lumbered after him, limping only slightly from his leg injury, and Petra followed, their soft sandals tapping loudly on the mosaics in the garden.

"Careful," he said, as they descended the stairs beyond the garden, "there's a blind corner near the servants' rooms below."

They slowed as they approached the kitchen, but it was deserted and smelled of death and rotten food. They moved toward the back, through a long hallway between rows of small house servants' rooms. As Petra came upon the first room, she noticed a barred door had replaced the original wooden door. She pushed it open and immediately recoiled at the sight of a blackened body crumpled against the far wall. She nearly retched from the sweet, rancid smell of burnt flesh.

Before she could react, Clarius knocked Lucius to the ground behind her and pushed her into the room with the corpse. She fell hard against the bed as Clarius slammed the barred door and slid a bolt across to lock her in.

By the time she was on her feet again, Lucius and Clarius were struggling with a dagger between them, each attempting to wrest it away from the other. She strained against the iron bars, hoping her new strength would bend them. They moved slightly, but not enough to let her squeeze through.

She looked up when the dagger Clarius had held inches from Lucius's face clattered across the floor. Clarius dove for it, scooping it up before rolling to the side to stab Lucius in the calf. He cried out from the pain but swung down to punch Clarius in the face. They rolled again, this time with Clarius on top. Lucius quickly began to buckle under Clarius's superior strength. Clarius turned the dagger downward, bringing it dangerously close to Lucius's heart.

"Fight him, Lucius. Fight for us!" Petra shouted.

Her words seemed to rally him, and he held Clarius at bay once again.

"So you decided to take my father's name, slave boy? You don't have the strength to fight me, *Lucipor*," Clarius said, emphasizing his slave name. "I am your master, and I will take her blood before this day is over."

Lucius glanced away for only a moment, his eyes meeting hers. When he brought his attention back to Clarius, it was too late. Clarius plunged the dagger into Lucius's chest, the movement excruciatingly slow. Lucius's scream ripped through Petra as she collapsed into the dirt-strewn floor of her prison. She screamed with him, her voice no more intelligible then an animal's cry of defeat when the predator delivers the killing blow to his prey.

As she stared at Lucius, watching him struggle with the pain, Clarius's laugh rang out like a death knell to her ears. He rose slowly to his feet, his eyes still on Lucius, who was gasping for breath. When he finally turned, the look of bloodlust on his face made her recoil.

"As you can see, I've already gone through all the servants, the slaves, the travelers on the road to Rome. I've been hungry for a long time, girl. Hungry, and waiting for my little Petra to make her way back home to her master."

Petra winced and backed away from him, trying not to think of the blood smearing the walls, the mosaics, and his blackened face. She forgot it all the moment she locked eyes with Lucius. He shook his head at her, unable to speak for the gasps that wracked his body. The blade's handle protruded from his chest, and the blade itself lay deep within his breast. How long did he have? Hours? Minutes? What if she didn't make it to him in time? She had to give him every moment she could. No matter what Clarius did to her, she would always rise again. But Lucius…

Clarius scoffed. "I am the one you have wronged, slave. Beg my forgiveness. Do as I say, and then I may let you live."

"You say this to a true immortal, Clarius. Something you can never be."

"What do you mean?" He narrowed his eyes at her, his anger lingering under the surface of his sneer.

She turned her chin up, refusing to answer.

"I seek an immortal's blood, then." He frowned at her, thinking. "I need your blood to survive, don't I, Petra? I've worked it out. That's why that boy looks as fresh as a lily flower, and I… Well, you don't look at me with quite the same fervor, do you? It wasn't the poison, after all. It was your blood."

Petra tried not to give the secret away. She kept her face a mask, but she saw it in his eyes. They both knew the truth now. There was no going back. It seemed like she had lost her last bit of leverage, and as she looked at Lucius, dying and in pain, she nearly gave up hope.

Clarius's corpse smile was grotesque. "I have you caged, my girl. I have an eternity to drink from you, have I not? I am sure I can find many ways to make you suffer… To make you die and rise again."

Petra's heart began to pound, but she did not give in to her fear. She would face him. She would let his black fingers touch her, his blood-stained mouth envelop her. She would force him to save Lucius's life.

"You don't know the truth about what you are. About what *we* are. You need me to give you the answers. Without them, you'll die." She took a deep breath and walked to the doorway, steadying her mind and her voice. She held onto the bars and nodded to him, beckoning him closer.

"You lie."

"Are you willing to take that chance?"

As she wanted, Clarius stepped closer to her. "Chance? I am no longer bound by chance. I am an immortal."

"No, Clarius, you are not. You are bound to me. Let me out of here or I will kill you."

He stalked forward, his smile arrogant. He made a grab for her through the bars, and she let him pull her against his body until they were face to face.

"I have you now, slave."

"No. *I* have *you*."

She began the draw from his heart, pulling with everything she had. The shock in his face almost made her smile, and the feel of his strength pouring into her as she watched the waves of pain flow through him made her feel powerful. It felt good to make him suffer, to see fear at last in *his* eyes.

"You are going to release me from this room, or I *will* kill you."

"Never."

Petra drew harder, until his arm fell away from hers, until his knees buckled. What she would never reveal is that his power and his strength were overwhelming her. He was far stronger than any human. Stronger than Lucius. Much stronger than Petra herself. She could only assume he gained that strength from all the lives he had taken, from all the blood he had drunk. She knew beyond a doubt that she wouldn't be able to kill him. Even now, her draw was weakening. She had to hurry.

"Let me out!"

He began to fiddle with the lock, his eyes wide, his pain intensifying. And then she was free. When the bars swung open, it broke her draw. So she slipped past Clarius and fell before Lucius.

"Go, Petra. Run!" Lucius said.

She sliced open her vein with the blade protruding from his chest. "No. I won't leave you. Now drink." Petra pressed her wrist to Lucius's mouth as she turned back to Clarius. It was all she could think to do to give him more time—maybe enough time to survive this day.

"Clarius," she said, evenly. "I offer you a proposition. Come to me once a year and no more. I will give you my blood in exchange for Lucius's life and a lasting peace between us." She hated saying the words. Hated that he existed. But she knew that neither of them could defeat him. So there was only one play left: surrender.

"You would offer yourself to me freely for that boy's life?"

"Yes."

Lucius pulled away from her wrist. "No, Petra. I won't allow it."

"It isn't your choice, Lucius." She hoped her tone would quiet him but he tried to rise, to pull at her arm.

"No—"

"Do you accept, Clarius?" Petra shouted, cutting off Lucius.

Clarius appeared to consider this. "You would… let me drink from you?" He narrowed his eyes at her even as he licked his lips. "I will kill you, you understand?"

"Yes." Her voice betrayed no fear, but she couldn't stop the revulsion from touching her eyes, disgusted by the mere thought of him taking any part of her—this murderer, this monster—into himself. She turned away, closing her eyes, feeling as though she were bargaining with Charon himself. Perhaps she was. If Clarius accepted, he would be the one carrying her to death; not just once, but every year for as long as she existed. She looked at Lucius's prone body as he slipped into unconsciousness. All Clarius had to do was leave her in this cell to watch Lucius slowly die without her life-giving blood. She had to tread carefully.

The expression on Clarius's face was one of anticipation, of longing. He looked at her as if she were his salvation and his next meal. It sickened her. At the same time, she understood why. She had felt this same madness, this rush of pleasure and pain. No other creatures on Earth had experienced a hunger like this. For other animals and humans, there was an instinct whispering to them that they must survive at all costs. But for her… and for Lucius and Clarius, they knew that they would wake again. There was a heady feeling in that sure knowledge for her. There was also a terror unlike any other as well. What if, as the years passed into decades and centuries, they did not want to go on living? Would they have the courage to end it all? Would they ever learn how it could be done?

She shook her head of her morbid thoughts and found that Clarius was staring at her.

"What of Silvipor? You will make him into what we are." It wasn't a question.

"You kept him alive?" she asked, eyebrows raised. That he would slaughter so many yet spare an insignificant slave said much to her about how much Clarius still valued him after all this time.

"I sent him away so I wouldn't kill him too. I want you to turn him into an immortal. I need someone loyal to do my bidding. Someone who will keep our secrets."

With begrudging acknowledgment, Petra realized he was right. She already knew Silvipor to be loyal to Clarius. The only reason that the master hadn't beat Silvipor as he did the rest of them was because he was his puppet among the slaves. The two had grown up together, and Master Clarius had always harbored a soft spot for Silvipor—likely because he dwarfed Clarius in size and fighting skill. Yet he had never opposed Clarius, and he always went along with the master's cruel pranks and punishments against the other slaves. As distasteful as it was to her, it seemed prudent to turn Silvipor rather than a stranger. At the least, Silvipor would keep his master's secrets and remain loyal.

She nodded. "If you must have a companion, I will turn him a year from now when you come to me again."

"Why only once a year?"

"We have learned it is all Lucius requires to live without desiccation. That is my bargain, Clarius. No more, no less. Do you accept?"

"You would live here?"

Her laugh was bitter. "In this house of depravity and death? Never."

Clarius began to shake his head, a sneer marring his blackened face.

She held up her hand. "We would not go far."

"No, you won't. I will have you watched. Try to run, and I will track you to the ends of the Earth."

"Petra, no. Don't—" Lucius called out to her, his words stopped short by a wracking cough. He rose slowly to a crouched position, his chest heaving from the pain. Blood did not pour from it, and she realized the dagger itself must be stopping the flow from the wound. It was likely keeping him alive as well. If the knife was pulled out, he would likely die even faster from the blood loss. Even now, he looked pale and weak as blood spilled from his mouth to the floor. But, still, he attempted to reach her.

"No, Lucius. Stay there." Then she withdrew, so that only Clarius could see her face. "What say you, Clarius. Will you accept what I offer or no?"

"Don't bargain with him, Petra. Better that I should die than you give yourself to him. Please." The weakness and pleading in Lucius's voice made her force back tears.

Better that I should, my love... I who can live forever.

"I accept," Clarius finally said, taking no notice of Lucius's pleading. "On this day one year from now you will send word, and I will come to you. Agreed?"

"Agreed." She was the one who brought this monster back to life. He should be food for maggots. Instead, it was her blood that had awakened him. It was she who was solely responsible for keeping her mother's murderer alive.

Lucius moaned at the sound of her acquiescence, but Clarius ignored him and took her by the wrist, his hideous skin making her step back. He laughed as she backed up against the wall, but he pulled her out into full view of Lucius.

"Don't make him watch this."

"Oh, I think he'll enjoy it," Clarius said, coaxing her with a gentle voice that unnerved her.

His hand felt rough against her skin. He forced her to kneel with him in front of Lucius, who reached out to her. He had never stopped shaking his head, even as he wheezed and his chest heaved with the pain. Clarius roughly grabbed both of her arms to force her to look at him.

"This is for the murder of my wife and child."

Then he pulled her to him, and Clarius's draw began. Petra cried out when his teeth penetrated the delicate skin of her neck. The exquisite pain was a shock, and it moved through her body, her blood, like a venom made of fire. She had no refuge from the pain, nowhere to hide. He drew back the power she had taken from him, drew, it felt, like the very essence of who she was. Then a change began, a cooling in her veins, a release from the torture. The pain began to subside, and it was replaced with a sickening pleasure. To her shame, she began to hope that he would never stop, never let go. Her cries of pain soon turned to moans of pleasure. When her vision clouded over, all Petra glimpsed was the darkness of the bathhouse, and all she remembered was the moment of her last death. The sound of rushing water assaulted her ears, but it was only the beat of her heart in time with Clarius's.

When he finally released her, she fell to the stone floor, her head lolling to the side. Her vision grew dim but what she saw ripped her heart in half: Lucius was staring at her, a look of pure horror on his face.

She tried to open her mouth to speak, but her body would not move. Clarius leaned over, blocking her last connection to Lucius. He drew near to her ear and whispered as her eyes closed and death began to take hold.

"Now I have had my taste of you, slave girl… and my revenge. When I come to you next, you will beg me to take you again."

She willed herself to die, then, wanting nothing more than to erase the memory of the pleasure he had wrought inside of her.

VIII

The Escape

August 13, 1 AD

PETRA WOKE TO THE SOUND OF RIPPLING WATER AND BIRDS WARBLING. SHE felt the cool of the open air. The only thought that came to her was whether her mother was already up at the master's villa to check on Constantia or if she needed to wake her. Petra rubbed at her eyes and took a deep breath.

Then the stench of death made her jolt to a sitting position. Everything came back to her in a rush. Clarius must have laid her body on the flagstones in the villa's garden. but he was gone now. Only the dead remained.

Lucius! Petra jumped to her feet. She ran down the stairs and found Lucius where Clarius had left him. Even before she dropped to his side, Petra saw that he yet breathed, but the blade remained deep inside him as he lay in a pool of his own blood.

"Lucius, can you hear me?"

He opened his eyes to her, but they were shot through with pain. He moaned and tried to cough up blood, but the effort left him weak as blood streamed from the corner of his mouth.

"We are free to leave, my love," she whispered, unable to check her tears. "Please, let me take you away from here."

"I can't move." He shifted against the hard stones, grimacing and breathing heavily.

"Here, let me pull the dagger out."

61

He shook his head. "I'll lose too much blood."

"Can you stand?"

"I Don't know." His words seemed to come a little easier now.

He cried out, and then sucked in a breath as she helped him to his feet. When he finally stood, he clung to her side. "Get me out of here," he whispered, his words barely audible.

Helping him negotiate the stairs proved far more difficult than helping him to rise.

"Drink from me," she said. "It will give you the strength you need."

"Soon," was all he would say.

She didn't understand, but he pressed on, so she did too.

They moved quietly through the various rooms of the house, Petra gingerly steering Lucius around the bodies, which lay in various states of decay. The sickly-sweet smell and the sight of decomposing flesh threatened to make her vomit. Lucius held to her tightly, his walking ability slowly diminishing.

As they moved through the *tablenum*, the master's finest room, they saw Clarius, surrounded by the dead. His skin was no longer ashen, his veins no longer black. He looked again as he had when he had been master of this grand and ancient villa. He held an empty bottle of wine against his temple and drank deeply from the goblet in his other hand. Petra was surprised by what she saw in his eyes: misery.

"You did this to me, slave girl. All of it. You made me poison my family. You turned me into a blood-sucking devil. And now… Now your blood has made me hate myself and everything I have become."

"Bury them all, Clarius," she told him, ignoring his words so she wouldn't have to feel pity for him. "Bury these people and sacrifice a pig to Ceres to sweep away all this madness."

"A madness you have wrought," he said, his voice as cold as the corpses around him. "If you want this to end"—he swept a hand over the dead—"you will keep our bargain. Attempt to escape so you can leave me here to die, and I will take my vengeance upon the world."

Though it made her ill, she said the words. "I will keep it."

He acknowledged her with his raised glass, saying only, "Until we meet again, slave girl," and then he turned away without another word as they passed him by.

She exchanged glances with Lucius. Blood began to stream from the corner of his mouth again as he doubled over with pain.

"Take me out into the light," he said.

"We are almost there," she whispered. "Hold on."

When the morning sun hit their faces, it washed away the horror of

Clarius's madness. They moved as spirits through the bodies of the dead, stumbling out of the villa and into the olive grove beyond.

There, Lucius collapsed at the foot of the nearest tree. His breathing grew more and more labored as his body slowly began to give up.

"Now, Petra," he said. "Pull—the dagger. Draw from me."

Petra didn't register his meaning. Her mouth gaped open, and she didn't think she had heard his halting words aright. When it finally dawned on her what he meant, she had only one question.

"Why?"

"I want you to take my life. Not Clarius."

His statement dumbfounded her but she understood. She would probably want the same if their roles were reversed.

"You are certain?"

"Remember old Tibullus, Petra."

She frowned in confusion, and then she remembered. Tibullus was one of his favorite poets. She spoke the words as her arms surrounded him: "May I be looking at you when my last hour has come, and dying may I hold you with my weakening hand."

"I will see you when I wake, my love," Lucius whispered.

"I will not fail you." When Petra wrenched the knife from his chest, Lucius's cry echoed through her body, and she shuddered along with him.

Petra drew his life as gently as she could, hoping to turn his pain into pleasure. He was so weakened by his injury that it didn't last long. They were locked together in the power of the draw, and only moments later, the vapor escaped from his wound, and she felt his heart stop.

She took up her dagger, and sucked in a breath as she opened a small cut in her neck. She held him close and raised his cool lips to skin untainted by Clarius.

"Drink, my love, and rise again."

63

IX

The Vellessentia

Rome

August 13, 2 AD

Petra reached out to Lucius, but he pulled away from her and rose from the bed.

"I cannot do it. I won't watch while he—"

She closed her eyes and sighed. He couldn't even say the words. How would they get through this every year for all of eternity?

"We have been over this too many times. You agreed."

"No, *you* agreed. With him."

"You know why."

Lucius sliced his hand through the air. "You should have let me die."

"So I would be alone forever without you?"

"So I wouldn't have to watch him murder you forever, Petra."

This brought her to her feet. She walked to him, pressed her fingers to both sides of his face.

"Clarius will not come between us. I won't allow it. He is our enemy, but you know as well as I do he is more powerful than the both of us. If we cannot kill him, we will quell him."

"What do you mean?"

"You saw it yourself when we left the villa. My blood changed him. It was the first time I have ever seen him regret anything in his whole life.

At least if he comes here, I will have some measure of control over his endless killing, and we will have a better chance of keeping our immortality a secret."

"Nothing will quell the monster inside him." Lucius's voice was quiet and measured, but Petra felt the anger reverberate beneath his words.

"I can. And I will." She moved away to dress. "I also think we need to start making our future plans."

"What do you mean?" Lucius donned his tunic, which was a far finer fabric than anything they could have ever dreamed of as slaves. In his blue linen, he looked more handsome than Clarius ever had in his expensive Chinese silk.

In the year since they left Clarius's villa, they had gone from owning nothing to acquiring a small estate on the outskirts of Rome. At first, they stole their way to financial freedom, their speed and quick reflexes becoming natural assets. They also found that humans were drawn to them now. Immortality had given them preternatural beauty, made their allure more seductive. They, too, were drawn to each other in ways that they could never have been as mortals. Senses heightened, bodies strong and lithe, they marveled at each other every day. Some days it took all their willpower to keep from drawing from one another. The desire had often overpowered Petra, but she was learning to control it over time.

They had begun to buy up fields and cultivate them into vineyards. They planned to sell high-quality wine to wealthy Romans, and they had the benefit of time to build for their future.

"There are only three of us in all the world, Lucius. We should create more like us. More Essentiae. I sense that Clarius will eventually ask me to do the same for those like him."

"Those that drink blood to kill? You must not—"

"You drink my blood," she countered, holding out her wrist.

"Only to survive. Only for life."

"You think I would freely offer Clarius an army of immortals? No, of course I wouldn't. But you know as well as I that he holds too much power. I cannot yet refuse him."

"Focus on what we could be to each other. To the world. If we had a family…"

"Who would want this life?" he asked.

She frowned. Did he regret being with her already? She shook her head in an attempt to hide how much his words stung. "Who wouldn't? There isn't a Roman out there who would deny themselves immortality if I offered it to them."

"What would be the purpose?"

"We don't have to merely exist. Think of all we could learn, of all the good we could do for the world. We had small lives before. We slaved for our master endlessly, day after day. Now the world lies at our feet, and we are only beginning to realize our potential."

"A beginning tainted by the thirst for blood and death."

"You will be the only one to let him come between us, Lucius. Clarius and I... You think that there is something between us. You've never asked me what it actually is."

Lucius frowned, waiting.

"It's hate, Lucius. I hate him."

"Can you hate him if you never loved him?" His voice was sharp, and she heard the fear tinging his words.

"Can you?" she demanded, her patience growing thin. "Yes, I can feel that he desires me. But it is my blood he wants. Nothing more."

"I saw it. I saw it in his face when he drank from you. I saw it in *your* face."

"No—" she started to protest, feeling uneasy with his line of questioning... remembering with shame the blood rush she had felt with Clarius.

"It was ecstasy... desire. You wanted him. You cannot deny it."

Petra stared at him, trying to think of a lie he would believe. "Gods, Lucius, I cannot. But you know what it is like to be in the throes of that madness. All reason flies from your mind and the body takes over. I was about to die. I could feel my life leaving me. You have felt that loss of control. You know..." She reached out, desperate to feel his arms around her, but he turned his back on her and moved toward the window to gaze out over the city. Rome was alight with the rising sun, but the tranquil scene couldn't quell her growing fear.

"I know. I know how much stronger my love for you became when you were drawing from me. That's what I lost control of, Petra. My love for you. It became a sickness, a desire that turned into despair for the wanting of you."

"It was that desire that bound us together." She moved to stand behind him and pressed her hand to his shoulder. "You were my first. You will always be first to me."

"Will it be enough for an eternity?"

"Yes." She kissed him, then, turning it into a gentle draw to remind him of the power only they held in all the world. "You are mine," she said simply, allowing the Essentian draw to ebb until it was only a kiss.

Lucius seized her close in his sudden need, and the curves of her body fit into his like a key to a lock. Perhaps that was his intent, to remind her that she was still his. His kiss deepened, roughened. He explored her mouth with his tongue, while his hands pulled at her hair. He pushed her down into the bed again, and she smiled.

"I will die today, Lucius, but you will give me a reason to rise again."

"Oh, yes, I will."

He slid her tunic from her body and ran his hand up her thigh and up to her breast, circling with his fingers before dipping his mouth to the supple skin of her throat. He bit her gently there, a reminder of what was to come… an unbidden memory of the desire she had felt when Clarius had taken her to heights she had never known, to the edge of madness and beyond.

Petra forced Lucius to look at her, forced herself to look at him.

"Love me," she whispered. "Love me until I can no longer remember his name."

Lucius's stunning brown eyes turned into liquid desire, and he entered her. Petra remembered again the stolen moments in the olive grove before immortality had touched them, when his fingers had fumbled under her tunic with a boy's clumsy desire, when his sloppy kisses had made her laugh. He told her they would run away together someday, and she had believed him. Petra remembered the boy in the man inside her, and she fell in love all over again.

"Love me," she whispered over and over, until the heights he brought her to went beyond all past and future. He brought her into the present, and on this day of all days, it was enough.

"Mistress, you have a visitor."

Petra studied Caelia's face. The servant girl seemed frightened. It must be Clarius come to collect his promised blood.

"Let him into the *triclinium* room, then. He is an important guest in this house, Caelia, and I will serve him myself. You will gather all the servants and see that they remain out of the house until tomorrow at this exact hour. Do you understand?" The last thing Petra needed was the cries of her death throes setting the servants' tongues to wagging.

After Caelia nodded and left the room, Petra glanced over at Lucius, who lay aside her in bed, propped up on one arm. He had been watching her.

She kissed him but could not seem to look him in the eye. Rising from their bed, she hurried to dress again and make herself presentable.

She knew he hadn't taken his eyes off her, but she didn't know what else to say to ease the wide river of distrust between them.

She wanted to tell him nothing could separate them, least of all their greatest enemy, but the words would not come. She turned her back to Lucius and closed her eyes to recover her equanimity. And she did. She resolved to beat Clarius at his own game tonight, to never relinquish her power. Let Clarius smell Lucius on her. Let him taste of Lucius when he touched her skin. Let him remember that she would never be his.

"What do you feel, Petra?" His words and eyes testified his agony.

"I still feel you inside me. When I wake again after this night is over, I want to feel you inside me once more."

She slipped from the room before Lucius could respond. She already knew what he would say, and she couldn't bear to hear it. They had not spoken of it, but she assumed Lucius would stay away during this first Vellessentia with Clarius.

Petra strode through the house with all the confidence of a master, watching her servants scatter and head toward the posticum and out across the fields toward the servants' quarters they had specially built far away from the main villa. She reminded herself that she did ultimately hold all the power here. Clarius would die without her, and he would do well to remember it.

As she approached the triclinium, she saw him lounging like a cat on one of the dining room's various couches. The servants had brought in grapes, wine, bread, and olive oil. He hadn't touched the food, but he sipped at the wine as if he hadn't a care in the world. It irritated her to see him there, invading her space, lazing comfortably on the couch she had lain on with Lucius just last night.

"Clarius." Petra couldn't keep the disdain from her voice and she didn't try. In sharp contrast to his appearance the last time she had seen him, he was a thing of beauty now, dressed in all the finery of his station, with bronzed skin that could rival that of the gods. Yet, his usually grey-blue eyes had already turned to silver, a clear sign that he was in need of her blood.

"Petra," he said too loudly, amusement flavoring his voice.

His body language said he was still playing the part of the master. Yet the last time she had seen him, she witnessed what she believed to be his remorse at killing all the innocents at his villa. Did he feel that guilt now, or had the loss of her blood over the past year slowly diminished that?

To steady her nerves, she poured herself a goblet of wine. He watched her every movement, but his gaze kept shifting to her neck.

"Your eyes," she blurted.

"Yes, it seems to be a symptom of… well, the need for more of your blood. A thirst you will soon quench, yes?"

Unchecked desire flowed through his gaze, and she looked away, feeling a queasy disgust threatening to overpower her carefully constructed façade of self-possession. Inside, she was crying out for Lucius to come and take her from this room, this villa, this country. But even if they tried to run from him, she knew that he would never stop hunting them. He wouldn't give up until he'd locked her away and killed Lucius.

"It's why you're here, isn't it?" She didn't hide the contempt from her voice.

"Yes." There was no apology in his answer.

She moved away from him, feeling suddenly vulnerable, suddenly afraid. She hadn't forgotten what he did to her mother. She would never forget.

"Where is Lucius?" Clarius glanced through the open doorway. "Will he be joining our—"

"No," she said abruptly, not wanting to hear what word he would use to characterize this madness.

"I see."

Clarius studied her face, looking for the reason why. Petra refused to give him so much as a hint. Yet she couldn't hide the reason from herself. She did want Lucius here. She didn't want to go through this alone. But how could she ask him to watch her die? To watch Clarius murder her? He would only try to stop them, and she couldn't blame him. She would do the same.

Petra didn't know when or how, but she knew she would figure out a way to defeat Clarius, to kill him once and for all. For now she must bide her time. She was still a fledgling immortal with no knowledge of the extent of Clarius's powers or her own.

"There are things we must discuss before we begin," she said. "This is a new era, Clarius. I am no longer yours, and you will not demand anything of me. Ask and perhaps I will give. But the master and the slave no longer exist between us. Do you understand?"

He couldn't bring himself to fully acquiesce, so he inclined his head and smiled instead. "My slave, Silvipor, is here. As agreed, you will turn him."

She nodded and Clarius looked pleased.

"Where is he?" she asked.

"He waits outside."

"Stay here. I will fetch him."

Clarius nodded. She left the room and immediately slumped against the wall by the door, letting out the breath she hadn't realized she was holding. She didn't know if she would make it through another moment of Clarius's presence. She wanted to stab him with a dagger until all her blood ran from his veins and he no longer carried a part of her inside him. Yet it was her blood that had silenced the murderer within. What madness her life had become. Why her? Why was she born with this strange curse?

"Silvipor?" she called out when she had opened the main door to the house.

"Clarius calls for me, girl?" He immediately rose from where he crouched against a stone wall at the front of the villa. He looked nearly the same as he did the last time she saw him. He wore his usual tunic and had that same bullish expression that made him look perpetually angry.

"You will call me mistress now, Silvipor. I am no longer a slave and Clarius will never again be my master."

He narrowed his eyes at her, obviously debating about whether Clarius would wish him to comply. "Yes, Mistress," he finally said, though his words were slow and forced.

"Do you understand what is happening here today? Do you understand what Clarius wants you to become?"

"Yes, Mistress."

"This life is a kind of immortality—but only so long as I offer it freely to you. Without me, you will die. Clarius will die. Do you understand this?"

"Yes, Mistress." Still, his words were forced through tight lips.

"We are enemies, and we likely always will be. You have chosen to follow Clarius. But to stay alive, you must not cross me. You now have two masters, Silvipor, and I do not envy you."

He shrugged. "Even if I wished to live a different life, Clarius would never allow it."

"Yes"—Petra offered him a half-smile—"you are right." She turned back into the house and he followed one step behind to where Clarius waited.

When they entered, Clarius grinned at his slave. "Are you ready for immortality?"

Silvipor's bulk took up the whole of the narrow doorway, and he looked down in obeisance as he murmured, "Yes, Master."

"Well, come in, then, and let us watch the goddess at her work. How do you do it, Petra? From the neck?" Clarius instantly moved toward his slave as a predator stalks his prey.

"Stop, Clarius," Petra nearly shouted, recoiling as Clarius licked his lips in anticipation, eyeing his slave as a meal rather than a man. She sensed Silvipor's fear, and while she couldn't stop Clarius indefinitely, she could talk Silvipor through the steps at least.

"You will die today, Silvio. When you awake, you will become one of us. It begins when you drink this liquid." She held up the phial hanging around her neck.

"What is it?" Clarius asked warily.

"It makes no matter," she retorted, but she saw in his eyes that he wouldn't give up.

"You will tell me now."

"Or?"

"Or our bargain ends. And you know exactly what that means."

She stared at him hard, thinking. It was a secret she had hoped to keep from him. She knew he would find out eventually. It was inevitable. She took a deep breath and let it out.

"Poison."

"Poison?" Clarius eyed the liquid and narrowed his eyes. "The poison that killed us?"

"Yes."

"What is it, truly? Hemlock?"

"No."

"Tell me," he demanded.

"We call it mortanine." Since it was only the name her mother gave the flower, a flower that otherwise had no name, Petra hoped that revelation wouldn't come back to haunt her in the end.

"Where does it come from? How is it made?"

"That, Clarius, you will never know."

He laughed at that. "I have an eternity to wheedle it out of you, girl. I am a patient man."

"No, you are not," she retorted, and then turned her attention back to Silvipor. "Once the poison takes effect, I will feed you my blood. It is this, and only this, which will revive you. When you wake, you will be one of us. Do you understand?"

He nodded.

"Clarius may consider you his slave, but to the Essentiae—my kind— you are a freed man. To us, you will now be known as Silvio."

Silvio glanced at Clarius, a questioning in his eyes. His master laughed.

"She can call you the god Jupiter for all I care. It matters not. You are my slave, Silvipor, and will be for eternity."

Silvio bowed in deference to his master, making his final choice—a choice she sensed he would ultimately regret. An eternity of servitude?

She would rather die. She tamped down the niggling remembrance that she, herself, had chosen to become a slave to Clarius's bloodlust. It might be on her terms, but it was still a kind of enslavement.

"So be it. Let us begin, then."

She held out the phial to Silvio, and with trembling fingers he reached out for the bottle, but Clarius slapped his hand away.

"I will drink him first." Clarius didn't look at Petra as he said the words. "I will drink him to the point of death before you give him the poison."

"Master, I—" Silvio backed away even as Clarius advanced.

"Clarius, stop!" Petra shouted.

But the immortal had become the animal again, and he neither heard nor saw anything but his prey. He was at Silvio's throat before the slave knew what was happening. He cried out as Clarius ripped into his neck, spilling blood down to his dust-caked tunic. The sound of Clarius's sucking and drinking made her want to run from the room. She would soon be next at this feast. It was almost worse to watch Clarius kill another and be unable to stop it. She knew what was coming. The pain... and the pleasure. She had already decided she would attempt to draw him as he drew from her. She wanted to see into his mind as she had done with Lucius, to glean whatever information she could from his memories and thoughts.

Silvio was moaning, his head lolling and his arms relaxing into the precious few moments of pleasure after the pain of the Sanguine draw subsided.

"You must stop or he will die." Petra waited for some sign that he heard her, but Clarius was deep in the draw, his mind focused on the kill.

She leaned down close but did not touch him. "If you want him by your side, Clarius, you will stop now. Kill him and he is gone from you for an eternity, and you will have no one."

This made Clarius stop. The hideous sound of his mouth prying free of Silvio's ravaged neck made her ill. He lifted his head, using his tongue to lick the blood from his teeth in a moment of sheer ecstasy.

"I want more," he said simply, letting Silvio drop to the stone floor with a thud. He trained his eyes on her, then, heavy as they were with desire and satiation. She had seen that look in Lucius's eyes when he pulled her into bed with him. To see that need in Clarius's face now was confusing and thrilling and terrifying. More than anything, she wanted Lucius here by her side, though he could do nothing but stand by and watch. No, no, Lucius was right. She couldn't make him do such a thing. It would be too cruel.

Silvio attempted to speak, but he could no longer formulate words. She had to act quickly before it was too late. Clarius had drawn too long and too deep.

Silvio stared at the poison, and she sensed his terror in the words he could not say.

"To answer the question you fear to ask, Silvio: yes. It will hurt. But you will survive in the end. I give you my word."

Silvio nodded and slowly downed the poison she put to his lips. As he coughed and sputtered against the bitter liquid, she pulled the dagger strapped to her leg from its sheath. She kept her eyes on Clarius as she put the blade to her wrist and sliced. She winced but was glad she did not cry out. He watched her every move, anticipation growing in his eyes.

Her blood poured into the cup, the dark stream mesmerizing Clarius. "Save some for me, my sweet."

"You deserve none," she retorted, but all the same, she wrapped her wrist in the white cloth strip the servants had left her to stop the bleeding.

"Here, let me help you with that," Clarius said, reaching out to tie the knot of her makeshift bandage. His closeness felt too intimate, his touch too familiar. Those same fingers had wielded the blade that cut her mother's throat and stabbed Lucius in the heart.

"No," she nearly shouted. "Don't touch me."

"As you wish." He glanced again at Silvio. "The change is starting."

"Give him my blood before he loses too much feeling in his jaw," she ordered Clarius as she struggled with the bandage. He brought the goblet to Silvio's lips, and made him gulp it down. He drank too fast, spewing the blood all over the floor and Clarius's finery. He did not seem to notice or care.

"I can't feel my face, Master." Silvio writhed with the effects of the poison.

Petra knew that pain well. Seeing the fear and the suffering on his face grow darker and deeper, she began to feel sorry for him.

"How much longer will it last?" Clarius asked, obviously more annoyed at the delay in his own pleasure than in concern for his servant.

"I don't know. Each time is different."

"Can you make it go faster? Give him more poison?"

"No, he's ingested more poison than you or I did."

"I could drink from him," Clarius said, his voice low as he licked his lips.

Petra shook her head, disgusted. "Do you want to die alongside him, Clarius?"

"I need you, woman. I need you now," he said, stalking toward her, desire burning in his eyes.

While she might have no love for Silvio, she knew intimately the pain he was experiencing. She only wished that kind of pain on one man, and that man wasn't Silvio. She decided, then, to hasten Silvio's death with an Essentian draw.

"I will try," she said. "Stay where you are. Don't come any closer."

Petra knelt at Silvio's side, who looked up at her with terrified eyes as his whole body shook with tremors. "Silvio, I am going to try to take the pain away. This will terrify you at first, and then you will begin to feel a kind of pleasure."

He did not respond because his face was fully paralyzed. So she leaned down to his lips and, without touching, began to draw him out. His eyes grew wider and wider as she drew deeper. She felt his physical strength passing into her, felt his falling away. She felt the connection waning and found herself wanting more and more of the taste of his power. At last she saw the pain etched on his face ebb into peace, but by the time she had grown aware of herself and where she was, he had died.

She pulled away from him, her breathing rapid, her body trembling from exertion.

"By the old gods, Petra. You will do this to me." It was not a question but a statement. She looked at Clarius, and the desire in his eyes shocked her.

"By the old gods, Clarius, *she will not*." Lucius had entered the room, and he towered over them all as they lay like corpses on the ground.

"Lucius, please." She begged him with her eyes to leave, but she knew what this gruesome scene must look like to him.

"Come to join us, I see," Clarius said with a smile Petra wanted to slap off his face.

"Stop," Petra warned.

"Or what? He'll kill me? We all know from past experience that isn't possible."

"Why are you turning Silvipor?" Lucius's anger at her was evident as he spit out the words.

"For our protection," she countered, as her breathing began to slow.

Lucius laughed bitterly. "Was that Clarius's excuse?"

"Please go, Lucius. You knew what had to happen here today."

"I did not agree to you turning him. I would never have agreed to it."

"We will discuss it later," she said, rising slowly.

"I have a question for Clarius. A question from one master to another." Lucius's tone and his words were not lost on her, and it annoyed her greatly.

75

"By all means," Clarius replied, obviously enjoying their quarrel.

"I am going to ask you something, Clarius, and I want you to answer with the truth."

Clarius's smile was slow and deliberate. He was more relaxed and calm than she had ever seen him. She realized that unnerved her most of all.

Lucius held up the goblet. "Can you drink her blood from a cup?"

"I cannot."

"Why?"

"I have attempted such, but it did not sate my lust."

"Or is that just what you want Petra to believe?" Lucius's mouth thinned into a line, and his anger grew as the moments passed.

"You remember the bodies at the villa, don't you, Lucipor? Some of those fell victim to my last attempt."

"I saw the worst of you, Clarius, the day you murdered my father. Nothing you could do would shock me now."

"A man of my… tastes needs far more than mere blood. I need the kill. Petra saw to that when she made me."

"As well you know, that was an accident," she reminded him.

"You both would do well to honor the bargain we struck."

"That *you* struck," Lucius said. "You bargained for me when I was unable to speak for myself."

"So you would have chosen death?" Clarius scoffed at this.

"Yes, I would have. You think I would willingly choose eternal death for the woman I love just to save myself? I am not so selfish or so cruel."

Lucius refused to look at her, even when she gasped at his words. She never truly understood how her bargain with Clarius had affected him. Knowing it now, seeing it through his eyes, would she have made the same choice again?

Yes.

Again and again and again.

If Lucius was by her side when she awoke, she knew she could endure an eternity of death.

"The only real power is survival, you fool. Some deserve life—the strongest, the most powerful. Others might as well die so the rest of us can get on with the business of living." Clarius looked at Petra. "Are you sure you don't want me to kill him for you now? He's merely a complication, is he not?"

"You will not touch him—today or any day. Not ever."

Clarius merely smiled.

"Lucius," Petra said, "go now. It will all be over soon." Despite her fear, she steadied and quieted her voice to try and tell him she understood why he had wanted to stay away. But he didn't hear the words she could not say. He only heard "Go."

"So be it."

The finality, the acceptance in Lucius's words carved a hollow place in her heart, a raw wound that burned like Sappho's fire.

Fill my heart with fire...

"Good, then." Clarius broke in, taking hold of her arm and forcing her to her knees. "It's time you gave yourself to me, Petra. I will be your Charon now, and the price for your passage is blood."

As Clarius drew her closer, his hand on her neck as gentle as a lover's, his silver-pale eyes dark with need, Lucius's eyes reflected his fall into defeat, into betrayal, into despair.

She wanted to scream at him to stay, to pull him into her arms and never let him go. But his words cut deep.

"I will leave you to your master, Petra, just as you wish." Lucius's fists shook with impotent rage as Clarius bit into her neck, making her gasp from the pain.

Stand by me and be my ally...

"Lucius, stop," she called, choking out the words as the blood rose in her throat.

He turned from her in disgust.

"Let go of me—" she demanded, but Clarius was the animal again. He held fast to her body, clinging to her as he tore into her viciously. Even as the blood began to rush between them, she heard Lucius's footsteps falling away, the sound drawing tears from her eyes.

The moment he left, the pain slammed into her. The fire in her veins, the sharp, stabbing pain, the fear... She let her body carry her loss of Lucius deep into the center of her chest. *Fill my heart with fire...*

Clarius pulled free long enough to beg her for an Essentian draw. She welcomed it, wanting to punish him with the same pain he inflicted on her.

Petra took hold of his head, her fingers digging into his skull, and she drew on him as hard as her waning strength would allow. His mind was so powerful it nearly compelled her hands away, but she held on, hoping to kill him before he could drain her fully. This time, she did not see images of Clarius's past life as she had with Lucius. Before the blood loss took the strength from her hands, she drew down deep into his mind and, as her pain diminished into the exquisite ecstasy of death, she glimpsed his thoughts: raw, unfiltered, seething.

Die, slave. Die and die again. I hate what you've done to me. For making me a slave to your blood. For stealing my birthright, for destroying everything my father built. I will make you suffer for an eternity. And, one day, I will master you again.

Petra broke from him, releasing herself from the horror of his dying thoughts. She screamed Lucius's name before the darkness took over, before Clarius drained her last drop. But Lucius did not come. Only the arms of her greatest enemy surrounded her, his words filling the emptiness in her veins where her blood had once run.

The Wounds

Sicily

February 21, 1723

"WHAT HORRORS YOU HAVE SURVIVED," AURELIA WHISPERED. "HOW DID you?" She looked at them both, marveling at their strength and courage.

"We did what we had to do," Lucius said.

"I've always thought you both as strong as the gods. Now I know you are."

Petra shook her head. "We had always hoped to find a way to quell Clarius for good long ago."

"Do you think we ever will?" Aurelia asked, dropping her quill into the inkwell.

"Perhaps someday we will discover the answer we seek, the secret of my blood. It hasn't been for lack of trying." Petra's frustrated smile dissolved into that ancient sadness again.

Lucius laid his hand atop Petra's, squeezing her fingers. "We will figure it out, and the new advances in science will pave the way. I'm sure of it."

Petra glanced at Aurelia, then, and she gave the lady a sad, knowing smile. They alone knew what was coming. It was what the two of them had used the Immortal Codex for all these years: to hide their plans behind her unbreakable cipher for a final war between the Essentiae and Clarius's *Sanguinea*. Petra was playing the long game, building a foolproof strategy over centuries. She would continue to build her army and fortify the Essentiae against Clarius's seemingly impenetrable strength. They had all long suspected the blood from his kills was the main source of his preternatural power. Their tests had proven it. What science could not tell them yet was why it gave him such dominance over them and how they might combat it. Petra was waiting for the answers in her blood before she would finally reveal her plans to Lucius. Aurelia also knew why. If Lucius had known her plans, he would have pushed for this war far too soon. And that Petra could not abide. She would never put any of them in that kind of risk.

Aurelia couldn't help the images flashing before her, images of Clarius there at Petra's throat on that first day of their immortal lives, pulling her toward him, his mouth desperate for her... Aurelia shuddered and looked again at Petra who gazed patiently at her.

"I am sorry, Madame. I was thinking again of Clarius's first draw." It was the moment that had started it all, when they had become locked in an endless feud with a promise sealed in blood.

"Has Clarius ever... Do you think he will ever let it go, this loss of his wife and child?"

"Never," Petra stated emphatically. "His memory is as long as mine, and our transgressions against each other run as deep as the blood in our veins. Even the yearly quelling does not seem to lessen that anger."

"He is who he is, and he will never change," Lucius said, not bothering to mask the bitterness in his tone.

"I remember his anger back at my first Vellessentia."

"Yes, I have much more to tell you before we get to that," Petra answered, as she settled back into her chair to resume her story. "I will now skip to the year we first met you."

"Thirteen forty-five in my beloved old Avignon," Aurelia said, smiling at the memory of that fateful moment when Petra and Lucius first whisked her away into the world beyond time.

"Yes." Petra glanced away from Lucius. "The year everything fell apart."

"The year *I* fell apart," he repeated, his words slow, his voice taking them all back there, back to where the wounds were as fresh as the day they were made and still burned as bright.

PART II

1345

Genoa, Italy

The Letters

Genoa

May 16, 1345

"WHAT HAVE YOU BEEN UP TO THIS TIME?" PETRA ASKED, WALKING INTO a disarray of glass shards all over the floor and work benches.

By the looks of it, Lucius had spent the entire night in his workshop. Petra shook her head and smiled. Since nearly the beginning of their lives together, she had seen him dive headlong into all manner of inventions. He loved building things, taking things apart and putting them back together. Yet, he was methodical about it, writing copious notes about all his current projects. She was glad it helped fill his endless days with new knowledge.

She craved knowledge, too, but in different ways. Science and ancient texts were her passions, but it was mastery of herself she sought most of all. She studied her blood meticulously, hoping to uncover the secret of her immortality. Her greatest hope was to discover a way to break Clarius's hold over her so they could finally destroy him once and for all.

Lucius looked up from eyeing multiple layers of glass secured with a vice. "I'm experimenting with spectacles."

"Need I remind you that you have perfect—and beautiful, I might add—eyes, courtesy of your lover?"

"Oh, no. I'm well-aware of that fact, *amor meus*. These experiments are merely a way to fill the hours."

She pulled his bearded chin toward her and kissed him until he had to catch her up in his arms when her knees buckled. He tasted of dust and honey wine, courtesy of the empty cup sitting next to two drooping candles.

"Are you tempting me to the bed I should have been in hours ago?"

"No, actually, I bear news to keep you here a little longer." Petra held up the two letters she had received by messenger overnight, one thin and hastily sealed and one a thicker scroll sagging under the weight of its heavy, thick wax seal. The dawn's light shone in through the shop windows to highlight the ornate signature of the letter's author.

"Have we come into an inheritance from a long-lost ancestor?"

"Once again, need I remind you that you have more money than the pope?"

"No, no. I am likewise well aware of that fact, *voluptas mea*."

"Well, then. We've finally received word from Guy de Chauliac."

"Who?"

"Merely Pope Clement the Sixth's personal physician."

"Ah, and what in the devil would we want with him? Surely, you know far more than this man ever could."

"Not quite. I may have more general knowledge than de Chauliac, but I haven't examined as many corpses as this physician. He also happens to be a premiere expert on poison antidotes."

"Ah. Why didn't you say so?"

"I'm saying so now. I'm also saying we are going to visit Monsieur Guy de Chauliac immediately, so your new spectacles will have to wait."

"You hope he'll create a mortanine antidote for us."

"Yes. It seems prudent. At some point, a future Essentiae novitiate may change their mind."

He frowned. "Future novitiate?"

"I've been thinking of turning more Essentiae now that we have finally settled on the rituals we want to use," she said.

She and Lucius had taken to calling themselves the Essentiae, mostly as a reminder to them all that they were not like Clarius. They might desire the life essence of humans, but they attempted with every breath not to act on that desire. And Petra consoled herself that at least they did not seek to drink the blood of their victims as Clarius did. She called him a Sanguine now. He lived on the blood of humans and so she called him what he was.

They had also painstakingly built a set of laws and rituals around her bloodletting. They had split the Vellessentia into four rituals, which took place only once a year on August 13. This was partly to keep the enclaves apart from each other to reduce in-fighting. But Petra was well aware that if Lucius spent any length of time in Clarius's vicinity, his temper would get the better of him.

If any immortals had broken any Essentiae or Sanguinea laws during the previous year, the *Vindicatio* Ritual, or punishment ritual, took place. In all their years, they had never had the need for a Vindicatio. She hoped they never would.

The *Aeternitescentia*, or initiation ritual, came next, which was the turning of any humans who wish to become immortals. They had only had one such ritual thus far.

The *Renascentia* Ritual was the rebirth ritual for both *eternae* groups. Each immortal would drink from Petra, which would restore their health for another year. It had an added effect for the Sanguinea: the Quelling. They had yet to understand it, but something in Petra's blood quelled the Sanguinea's desire for the kill. It kept all of them safe from discovery, so she was grateful to offer her blood to the Sanguinea every year.

The final ritual was the Vellessentia itself, or the drawing of any immortals who wish to gain skill or knowledge from another immortal. They had yet to attempt this ritual. Petra wanted to study the phenomenon more carefully before they began to use it. She also worried that if Clarius learned of it, he would use it against them, passing strengths among his Sanguinea over the centuries to make them even more superior to the Essentiae.

These carefully cultivated rituals kept Clarius and his Sanguinea in check, and reminded them all of Petra's ultimate authority over both eternae, a carefully orchestrated set of rites that both protected and empowered her.

"What—as servants? Tired of hiding in plain sight among your human servants after twelve centuries?"

"Well, yes, if you must know, and also…" She didn't quite know how to break the news of the second letter.

"And?" Lucius prompted.

Petra held out the second letter to him. Let Clarius reveal this bit of news through his own words.

Lucius's eyes narrowed as he read the signature scratched at the bottom. When he finished reading the note, he held the edge of the paper to a nearby candle, and they both silently watched it burn to ash.

When there was nothing left to burn, he slowly turned toward her. "So your dear Clarius seeks a new member for his blood cult, I see."

"This is one of many such letters he has sent asking me to turn more Sanguinea for him." Beyond his longtime slave, Silvio, she had turned one other: a Japanese samurai and sword expert she renamed Nicon Matsuda.

"Clarius wasn't asking. He was demanding."

"Yes," she admitted, swallowing the sigh threatening to escape from her mouth. It made her wonder if Clarius had plans for this new immortal, plans to overthrow her. She had to tread carefully.

He said nothing in response, but she did not miss the tightening of his lips or his white-knuckled grip on the chair as he turned to blow out the various candles littering the worktable, most of which had burned dangerously low.

"This is our chance to even out the numbers, Lucius."

"With servants?" He raised his eyebrows.

"No. I mean to seek out the most brilliant minds and strongest of bodies the world has to offer."

Lucius ran his fingers over his lips, contemplating the idea.

"Yes, we do have a whole world to choose from. We could bide our time, wait for the brightest minds and the strongest of men—"

"And women," she said with a rueful smile, carefully omitting that her ultimate goal was to build an Essentiae army that would eventually destroy Clarius. Despite the passing centuries, she had never forgotten the thoughts she had glimpsed in Clarius's head of his hatred for her, of his desire for her death. But to reveal it to Lucius would put them all in danger. If he knew, if she ever foolishly let it slip, he would not stop until either he or Clarius were dead.

"Of course." Lucius grinned back, unaware of the dark thoughts rushing through her head. "I think it's brilliant."

"Let's discuss it on our way to Avignon, then," she replied, forcing a smile. For years she had secretly looked for a man with skill in encrypting text. She had long since recorded the histories of their centuries together as a testament to their lives, their adventures, their endless searching for the answers in her blood, their love. Yet she must turn her mind to a future hidden from all. A future full of plans to take down Clarius once and for all. First she had to find someone to help her hide her strategies—from Clarius *and* Lucius.

"This physician is at the Papal Palace in France?" Lucius asked.

"Yes, Guy de Chauliac goes wherever Pope Clement goes."

"And I go wherever you go."

"Almost." She hadn't meant to say it so soon, but there was no help for it. She would ask and he would have to agree. She would brook no refusal this time.

He didn't respond, but the muscle in his jaw tightened as he exited the workshop.

"Lucius, wait." She took his hand as he tried to pass her. He looked back, and she saw he was already tensing up.

"It's been centuries upon centuries," she began, knowing this conversation would likely end in shouts. "I want you with me at the Vellessentia this year."

He scowled. "After all this time…? What's changed? Why now?"

"As you saw from his letter, Clarius has revealed nothing about this novitiate he wants me to turn. I have no idea who this person is. I need you by my side in case something goes wrong."

"I've told you before—" He sliced a hand through the air, a clear sign he wanted to end the conversation immediately.

Frustrated, she clenched her fists, an anger that had been growing for centuries suddenly igniting. "No. You never want to talk about this. You never talk about our first Vellessentia. About Clarius. You can't keep pretending they don't exist."

"Pretending? Is that what you think I'm doing?"

"I don't know. Tell me, then. Tell me the truth. Why won't you come with me?"

Lucius drew his lips into a straight line, saying nothing.

She waited a moment more, hoping he would finally tell her. He only stared at her, anger flashing in his brilliant brown eyes.

"Clarius is different now. He's—"

Lucius turned on his heel and stalked off. "That bastard deserves no more than a slit throat and a funeral pyre."

Petra followed him, matching his pace. "You haven't seen him since the old days. He's changed."

"I don't believe that's possible."

"You doubt me?"

"I doubt him."

Petra shook her head, her frustration mounting. "How does it look when the only other Essentiae will not attend the Vellessentiae rituals? We created them together. I need you by my side."

He narrowed his eyes at her. "I refuse to watch him kill you."

"Don't think of it that way. You'd be coming for me. To help me. You don't know what it's been like all these years."

"I know. I haven't forgotten the last time. It's seared into my memory forever. I see it in my mind every year without fail. The images of… of what he did to you never leave me."

"I must have you there. I must. Don't make me beg you. Don't make me go through this alone even one more year."

He stopped abruptly, and turned from her again, staring off across their vineyards lit by the rising sun. "I love you too much, Petra."

"Then love me enough to be by my side. I need you, Lucius. I'm tired of missing you. I'm tired of being afraid. You owe me."

Lucius had begun to move again, but this gave him pause. Still he would not look at her. Still, he kept her at a distance. And he stood unmoving for several moments more. When his shoulders slumped, when he wiped a hand over his face and he blew out a long breath, she knew.

"You win, Petra," he finally said, pushing past her outstretched hand and stalking off.

Something in the way he said it broke her. There was resignation in his voice, but she also detected the unmistakable quietness of horror.

II

The Physician

Avignon, France

May 29, 1345

WEARY OF SITTING A HORSE AT A DRIVING PACE FOR THIRTEEN DAYS through all manner of spring rainstorms—and stormy looks from Lucius—Petra walked ahead on stiff legs toward the forbidding Palais des Papes in southern France. The bright limestone walls of the palace did nothing to allay her sense of foreboding, nor did the clearing storm clouds give her a sense of ease. Would de Chauliac have the answers they sought? She rubbed the phial at her neck and glanced back at Lucius. He looked as exhausted as she felt. What if mortanine had no true antidote and this was a fool's errand?

A portly, bearded guard approached them as they climbed the steps to the main gate. Workers milled about the main entrance, which was in a state of extensive expansion. Apparently this pope had grand plans for a more elaborate palace away from Rome.

"State your business," the guard said gruffly, pulling self-consciously at his whiskers.

"We have been summoned by Physician de Chauliac." Lucius held out the letter, which the guard snatched from his hand and perused for de Chauliac's seal and signature.

"His summons is of a medicinal nature?"

"Yes, Monsieur."

"The physician is expecting you?"

"Yes, though he was not aware we would arrive today."

"Stay here. I will fetch a page to inform him you are here."

"Thank you, Monsieur," Lucius said.

The wait was a long hour, but as the sun began its descension amid the fading clouds, a page finally came out to greet them. He pointed out the various sections of the formidable palace as they walked across the Il Cortile d'Onore where light rain began to fall onto the courtyard stones and all manner of elaborately dressed priests milling about. Eventually, they entered the far wing via the Salle de Jésus. Just past the old chamberlain's quarters they arrived at a small office. Here they were shown into a cramped but well-organized room doubling as a small library and laboratory. In the back corner, a scribe was sketching out a set of physician's tools into a book while Guy de Chauliac himself stood with his back to them, bending over what looked to be a delicate experiment.

The page cleared his throat. "Physician de Chauliac, your visitors, Monsieur Lucius and Madame Petra Valerii, have arrived."

"Thank you, Geoffroi. You may go," he said without looking up from his experiment.

It reminded Petra of Lucius when he was deep into his work and unable to tear his mind away when she would interrupt him with a kiss or a summons to bed. She glanced at him, the smile the fond memory created fading in the face of the anger lacing his preternatural features.

They waited a moment longer, and then the physician turned to greet them.

"So this is the mysterious Petra who has a poison that cannot be named."

He peered at her through a pair of round glasses that made him appear comically peevish even though a smile of amusement touched his features. He sported an expertly coifed beard with dark curls framing a face untouched by war or disease.

"Thank you for seeing us, Monsieur de Chauliac." Petra inclined her head by way of greeting and smiled.

He held up a hand. "Please, Madame, you must call me Guido. We stand on no ceremony here in this old back office. Do we, Roland?" he asked the scribe. The young, thin man smiled and shook his head. He resumed his painstaking drawing after acknowledging Lucius and Petra. "I'm sure you are most anxious to have your questions answered after traveling all this way."

Guido came around the counter after giving them a closer look. As she had predicted, the physician was completely disarmed by her appearance.

"And who is this gentleman, Madame?" he asked.

"I am Lucius, Petra's husband, Monsieur."

Guido leaned forward to peer at him in the low candlelight.

"You both have magnificent eyes. I have never seen their equal. Your skin... alabaster spun with gold. Where again do you hail from?"

"All over Italy, Monsieur." Petra's smile left him with his mouth agape. "We come from old Roman stock."

"It's a wonder you do not fear to come to me here, Madame. Our peoples are at odds these days, no?"

"We keep out of the war news from the north," Lucius offered, attempting a smile but falling short. "We live a quiet life in the country tending to our vineyards."

"Well, I would say country life has done you good, Madame et Monsieur!"

"Thank you," Petra said, rummaging in Lucius's pack for the large glass phial of mortanine and handing it to him. "We brought the substance with us. I created as much as I could so you would have enough with which to test and experiment."

"Well, well, let me see you now, little one," he said, as he walked over to peer at it nearer to the candles. "I shall call you Liquid X since your caretakers refuse to give me your name." He glanced back at them with a chiding amusement.

"It is rather that this liquid has no name. We picked it out of obscurity, and it is known only to us."

"What have you used this poison for, if I may ask? You do, after all, bring it here to the Palais des Papes."

"Not such a curious thing, Monsieur," Lucius said, "since Petra tells me you are an expert in poisons and their antidotes, yes?"

"Such is true, of course."

"We use it to control the rat population around our villa. We thought it best to see if there might be an antidote in case it is accidentally ingested by a human—and being a woman with interest in the sciences, I am curious about its general properties as well."

This surprised Guido, as evidenced by his raised eyebrows and temporary muteness. Eventually he nodded. "I confess your cryptic letter intrigued me. I will study this poison for you—under one condition."

Petra kept her expression passive. "What would that be, Guido?" she said, using his forename purposely.

"I wish to list this among the poisons in my collection and keep a small phial of it for further study. I would give it a proper name as well."

Lucius glanced at Petra, questioning the wisdom in giving this man free rein over such a secret. She shook her head slightly.

"Agreed, Monsieur," Petra said without hesitation. "How long will it take for you to assess whether there is an antidote?"

"Give me a couple days. The good thing about poisons is they work fast, no?" He laughed at his joke, though Lucius and Petra did not. They knew the answer to that firsthand.

"Did you happen to bring the plant from which you drew the poison?"

"I am sorry. I did not."

"Pity. This would have aided me greatly."

"I can tell you it came from a flower growing in central Europe."

"Excellent. Tell the page where I may find you. I will seek you out when my work is finished."

"Thank you for your assistance, Guido." Lucius bowed slightly.

"And thank you for bringing me an intriguing new project."

At that moment, the door opened and a young woman burst into the office. She held papers in her hand, some of which fell to the floor like feathers from a dove.

"You and Adélaïs are both of a similar mind, I imagine," the physician said to Petra as the girl ran straight past them in breathless excitement.

"You won't believe it, Uncle Guido. I cracked the cipher!"

"Ah, indeed?" Guido glanced at the paper she waved in front of his face. "You may have a brain the size of a country, *mon ange*, but you have forgotten your manners, it seems."

She glanced back at them, and Petra laughed at her expression.

"*Pardonnez-moi*, Madame et Monsieur. I confess I did not notice you there."

It was obvious their brilliant eyes had caught her attention—particularly Lucius's. He smiled at her, asking, "A cipher, you say?"

"Yes, Monsieur. To pass the time, my uncle gives me puzzles and science and language problems to solve. This week's was to solve a substitution cipher written by the famous Arab, Ali Ibn Muhammad Ibn Al-Durayhim." Her charming smile grew into a wide grin. "I cracked it."

Guido came to stand behind the girl, who couldn't have been much younger than Petra when she was first turned.

"Adélaïs here has a mind sharper than my own. If she had been born a boy, I would have snatched her up as my apprentice. As it is, I amuse her with games so she won't upstage my experiments with her own solutions!"

Adélaïs's smile was infectious as she leaned into her uncle and attempted to organize the papers in her hand. Lucius bent to pick up the pages she had dropped and leaned over to hand them to her.

"Well, it sounds like you would be an asset to anyone privileged to know you, Mademoiselle," Lucius said, and his glance at Petra made her realize he was talking to her instead. Instantly, Petra saw that Adélaïs could be the one to assist her in creating a codex of their immortal histories and her future war plans.

"Thank you, Monsieur," the young woman said shyly. "You are most kind."

"Adélaïs, meet Monsieur Lucius and Madame Petra. They have traveled all the way from Italy to seek my advice on an antidote."

Her eyes widened as she curtsied. "You must live in a land of endless sea and sun."

"Yes, we've had no rain for some weeks back at our villa. Summer nearly is upon us."

"I envy you. We've had nothing but rain for weeks here."

"Shall we return here to the palais for the results of your testing?"

"Certainly." The physician nodded. "Let the page know where he may deliver my summons. Give me three days."

"Agreed. It was wonderful to meet you both," Petra said. "We look forward to seeing the results."

As they made their way out of Guido's study, Petra overheard the physician speaking to Adélaïs.

"And, you, young lady, need to go home before the sun goes down. Your mother will worry."

"We would be happy to walk Adélaïs home, Monsieur, if she would but show us the way." Lucius ducked his head back into the study, his smile relaxed and cordial.

"Oh, I wouldn't want to delay your evening plans, Monsieur," Guido said. "Since Adélaïs is here most every day, I often send her home on her own."

"It is no trouble at all. We had planned to wander the city some anyway."

"I thank you for your kindness, Monsieur. I am sure Adélaïs would enjoy the company."

Adélaïs nodded with a smile that charmed them all.

"It is our honor. We will see her safely home, Monsieur de Chauliac."

"It's Guido, remember? Oh, and Adélaïs, I have an herb I want you to give your father. Come with me so I may give instruction on its use. We won't be a moment, Monsieur et Madame."

Petra and Lucius waited out in the hall.

"You were thinking the girl may be of use to us?" Petra whispered.

"Yes, it occurred to me she could keep your scribblings safe from prying eyes."

She glanced at him sideways, mildly annoyed. "They aren't scribblings. They are our immortal histories. It's not like you'd ever have the patience for it."

"Of course I have the patience. I just don't see the point."

"When have you ever seen me doing anything frivolous?"

"Never, actually." He reached over to squeeze her into an embrace, and she wondered, then, if his anger was starting to fade at last. "You're quite right. Perhaps it's your old age"—she slapped his arm for that transgression—"but you do have the most pragmatic mind I've ever encountered."

"My pragmatism would warn you to never discuss a woman's age."

"Noted. How should we broach this subject with her...?" Lucius asked. "Perhaps that we would like more information on a cipher for a book we would like to create?"

"Yes, that might work. Even if she relays what we say to her uncle, it wouldn't seem too far-fetched."

"Let's hope she doesn't mention it. If we end up taking her, he will alert the authorities of our presence in Avignon. It would be simple for him to find our residence in Italy."

"We may have to move if we keep her," Petra said.

"I hope not, but we should be open to the possibility."

"If it becomes a necessity, where would you want to go?" she asked.

"Somewhere nearer to the sea. I am craving the salt air."

"Southern Italy? Or perhaps a different country altogether?"

"First, we need to find out if this girl is as intelligent as her uncle says she is."

"We're about to find out," Petra whispered as Adélaïs entered the hall.

"Are you ready, Mademoiselle?" Lucius asked.

"Oui, Monsieur..." Adélaïs shook her head, presumably to force herself not to stare into his mesmerizing eyes. Petra knew exactly how she felt. She'd had to do that for centuries. Petra smiled as she took up his arm. She felt his draw even now, but she held fast, and whispered into his ear, "Tonight, you're mine. And as you know, I always get my way."

III

The Girl

May 30, 1345

THE THREE OF THEM HEADED OUT INTO THE CITY, TRAVERSING DOWN A narrow cobblestone street near an old aqueduct, as Lucius and Petra listened to Adélaïs talk about the encryption puzzles she had done for her uncle. Her eyes lit up with true excitement, which made Petra more and more certain she would be an asset to the Essentiae—and the first immortal for her future army.

"What aspect of puzzles and ciphers intrigues you, Mademoiselle?" Lucius asked.

"I don't quite know, to be honest, Monsieur. They've always fascinated me, even before my uncle introduced me to science and mathématiques."

"Does your uncle or your family have any future plans already decided for you? A marriage?"

"Oh, no, Madame. They have all agreed no man would want a girl with such an education. It would bring shame upon him."

Petra and Lucius exchanged amused glances.

"What, then, will you do?" Lucius pressed gently.

"I suppose I will care for my parents in their old age. I am not the eldest, after all."

The girl looked down at her scuffed boots, then, but Petra lifted her chin.

"If the world lay at your feet and nothing—not even the fact that you're a girl—stood in your way, what would you want to do with the rest

95

of your life?" Petra held Adélaïs's gaze, though fear leapt into her eyes. They stood there, locked together as the girl slowly drew up her courage to dream.

"I would travel the world, advising kings and popes and writing their missives. I would be an emissary. And I would never be afraid of anything anymore."

Petra nodded, knowing with certainty this girl would serve her well. She glanced up at Lucius, and she realized he agreed.

"Adélaïs, we have a proposition for you. Something you couldn't conjure up in your wildest dreams. A profound gift. A chance at all you desire. But all such things come with a price. If you wish to learn more, you must say farewell to your life as you know it and to those you hold dear."

The girl frowned. "How can such a thing…? Why me?"

"It is your mind we seek, Adélaïs. Your curiosity."

"Of all the great minds in the world?"

"Yes, yours. We have particular need of a codex for our library, and your skill will help us achieve that. Remember, if you decide to join us, you would have to leave your life behind. Not everyone has the courage to do so. So many things weigh people down: family, poverty, love, marriage. It will be your choice, but once you leave, you can never come back."

"Not even to visit?"

"Never, *ma chère*," Petra said with a quiet but firm tone.

"How old are you, girl?" Lucius asked.

"I am nearly eighteen."

"Old enough to make decisions about your own life, then."

"Yes, I suppose. Though I should like to consult with my uncle. He will know—"

"I am sorry, Adélaïs, but you cannot breathe a word to your uncle about what we've talked about here today. It would be dangerous for you and your family."

"I understand," she said, as she approached the stoop leading up to her family's house. "What would I be required to do?"

"I would need you to create a cipher for a codex I am writing."

"From scratch?"

"Yes, your very own cipher, one only you and I would ever know or be able to read. This codex is meant to be secret from all the world."

"What would be in the codex?"

"Ah, that I cannot tell you until you agree to leave your life behind and come with us."

"May I have time to think it over, Madame?"

"Yes, you have until your uncle comes back to us with his findings. I know this is sudden. We had no idea we would find someone so perfect for our needs when we came here."

"Will I be paid?" the girl asked.

"Yes and no. You will have no wage, and yet you will never lack for anything for all the rest of your days. Money will simply become irrelevant."

Adélaïs's eyes widened. "Would I be able to send money back to my family as compensation for my loss?"

Lucius glanced at Petra who nodded at the question in his eyes. "This can be arranged, Mademoiselle, as long as your family does not know the money has come from you."

"If I decide to come with you, how will I let you know?"

"On the night of the day your uncle gives us his findings, wait for us at dusk by the fountain beneath the Cathédrale Notre-Dame des Doms d'Avignon. You know it, no?"

"Oh, yes. We attend mass at the cathedral every week, of course."

"You would not need to bring anything with you, save any keepsakes you cannot part with. We will provide for your every need for the rest of your life."

"This seems like a dream."

"Frankly, the truth of who and what we are is far more than you could ever dream. If you come to the fountain, we will reveal all to you. Until then, think on what we've discussed but tell no one. We know this is no easy decision we put before you."

"Yes, Madame. Would we go to your home in Italy?"

"Possibly. We travel a great deal, and we move from time to time. Go now and think over what we have said carefully."

Adélaïs nodded and slowly walked up the steps toward her house. She knew the girl was thinking through the different ramifications and possibilities of what such a life might look like, as she would one of her ciphers or puzzles.

Petra didn't envy the girl. She, herself, had had no choice. There was some comfort in that. The girl's real decision would come at the fountain, when she learned the whole terrifying and magnificent truth. To look an eternity in the eye at seventeen years old… What would the girl do? And what would they do if she refused?

One thing was for certain, they could not let Guy de Chauliac relay anything about them to Pope Clement VI. They would be hunted to the ends of the Earth as abominations. No, Petra knew in her heart she would have to kill the girl if she refused to join the Essentiae. The danger was far too great to let her live with such a powerful secret.

IV

The Choice

"Y OU HAVE NEWS FOR US, MONSIEUR DE CHAULIAC?" PETRA ASKED.
"None that will give you comfort, I'm afraid, Madame."
"Oh?"

"I found no antidote for our mysterious Liquid X." The physician paused, folding his hands in front of him as he leaned over his desk. "I do apologize I don't have better news for you."

"It's quite all right. It is enough to know how dangerous it is."

"I *can* tell you it has similar properties to aconitum."

"Wolfsbane?"

"Yes," the physician said. "In my tests on rats, this poison caused erratic heart rates and numbness in the head and limbs."

"This was my assessment as well," Petra said.

"I would have to do more testing to discover more effects. In any case, I would caution you not to use this poison. There are other poisons with proven antidotes. For example—"

"No, no, you are quite right, sir," Petra interrupted. "It is good to know this poison is more dangerous than we first thought. We will take care to remove it from our home so as not to put ourselves or our servants in inadvertent danger."

"Yes, I strongly advise such action. Is there anything else you wished to ask me before we conclude our business?"

"I did have one question, Monsieur," Lucius said, "Have you ever studied human longevity?"

The physician frowned. "In what way?"

"Do you know what causes some people to live longer than others?"

"I confess my areas of study have been confined to anatomy, anesthetics, wounds, fractures and, of course, antidotes. It does, however, sound like a fascinating area of study. You might ask an alchemist. They are those singular creatures concerned with what could be rather than what is."

"Indeed. It's always been an area of interest to me," Lucius said. "I may do my own personal studies on the subject to see what more I may learn."

"I would love to see your research if you do embark on such an adventure. If you find the key to immortality, I know a great many popes and generals and kings who would be interested in such a discovery!"

The physician laughed, amused at his own joke. He failed to notice Petra and Lucius did not join him.

That night, Petra and Lucius waited in the shadows by the fountain beneath the colossal Cathédrale Notre-Dame des Doms d'Avignon. Dusk had long since fallen and a thick fog had descended around the cold stones of the grand Palais des Papes, but the girl was nowhere to be seen in the thinning crowds. Black-robed priests walked in groups from the cathedral to the palace as the day's ecclesiastical activities wound down. Families hurried by as well as construction workers heading home from a long day's work.

"Will she come, do you think?" Lucius asked her.

"I worry her family will catch her leaving and force her to stay home."

"As do I."

They waited half an hour longer, and then they saw Adélaïs's slight figure wrapped in a heavy cloak and scarf emerging from the fog across the lower square.

"Now we will see what comes of young Adélaïs's fate," Lucius said.

Petra nodded, hoping she would choose the Essentiae over death. When Adélaïs reached them, she was breathless from her run, but in the hazy lamplight above, they saw the light of excitement in her eyes.

"So you decided to join us after all, Mademoiselle," Lucius said.

"I thought long and hard about all you have said. I weighed the possibilities against the loss of my family. I realized I would regret it for the rest of my life if I did not say yes to your generous offer."

"You will not be disappointed, Adélaïs," Petra said, yet she did not hide the warning tone in her voice. "But you will be shocked when you learn the whole truth. Sit here at the fountain's edge while we tell you about what we are."

The girl frowned, but she did as she was told. She set down the small bag of belongings she had brought and settled against the cold stones, her back against the wall leading up to the square in front of the cathedral. They sat down beside her.

Lucius began without preamble. "We are immortals, Adélaïs. We have been alive since the days of Ancient Rome, before the turn of the millennium, and we have no reason to doubt we will remain as you see us now for the rest of eternity."

Adélaïs was struck dumb for several long minutes. She opened her mouth to speak, and then immediately shut it again, and all the while Petra watched as the concept slowly settled into the girl's mind, as a new reality to replace the old, just as she might incorporate new teachings from her uncle into her daily study.

At last, Adélaïs said, "How did this come to be?"

"We still don't have all the answers, even after all this time," Lucius said, his voice gentle but firm. "But it is Petra who is the source of our immortality."

Adélaïs shied slightly away from them, her gaze darting around to see if anyone nearby overheard.

"It is an element in her blood that turned us into what we are, but she is the true immortal, the one who can never die."

"When you say 'us...' There are others like you?"

"Yes. Several." Lucius gazed at Petra as he said these words, and in his eyes were all the unspoken arguments they had ever had about Clarius.

"Adélaïs," Petra said, taking hold of her hand gently, "we are offering you a life that will never end. Our eternae—we call ourselves the Essentiae—is small. It is just the two of us, Lucius and me. You would be our third. Immortality came to us by accident, but you will be the first of our *eternae*, our enclave, to choose eternity for yourself. You can walk away if you wish it."

As Petra said the words, she realized there was no real choice. The girl would either choose to become an immortal or they would have to kill her. Letting her go would be far too dangerous.

Again, the girl was silent. Then she looked up at Petra. "What is it like to live forever? To live without fear of death?"

Petra smiled. "I have lived this way for so long, it is hard to remember what it was like to live as a mortal. I would put it this way: we live in a world without time. We savor the moments of life, but we do not treasure them in the same way you do. Having all the time in the world means you may pursue any passion that pleases you, but I would say it takes a strong person not to succumb to ennui, to boredom, to despair. What makes this heavy weight of time bearable is living our lives together."

"Death is not possible for you?"

"You remember what Lucius told you about my blood?"

Adélaïs nodded.

"No, I cannot truly die. My blood is a restorative of sorts. Even if you died—and you may well die from time to time—my blood can bring you back to life."

"How strange to hear you talk of death as if it were merely temporary."

"For us, it is," Lucius said. "It does not last, and we have yet to see its effects remain permanently within us."

"That is not to say you and Lucius could not die and remain thus. That is possible, so far as we know. If ever you decide you have had enough of life, you would simply not take the blood I freely offer you."

"Blood?"

"This is one aspect of our lives you may find disturbing. You can only live if you ingest my blood at least once a year. It will keep you strong, help you heal from injuries, and keep you free from disease."

Adélaïs glanced up, toward the cathedral above them, and crossed herself again. "Surely, such a thing would go against God's commandments, against the teachings of the priests—"

"That I cannot say," Petra said. "They have no knowledge of us. Our understanding of ourselves is still in its infancy."

"It isn't for lack of study, Adélaïs." Lucius pressed his hand over Petra's. "She has dedicated her life to the study of our kind, to learn all she can about what we are."

"How would I become what you are?" Adélaïs said, her voice tinged with worry.

Petra couldn't keep the sadness from her smile. "Do you remember the liquid we gave to your uncle? That is a poison we call mortanine. This liquid would kill your mortal body, and my blood would help you rise into immortality."

Adélaïs gasped. "I would have to die to become like you?"

"Yes," Lucius said, "but it is only mortal death. I have died more times than I can count—and Petra far more—but we always come back stronger than before."

"You would change, Adélaïs," Petra explained. "You would be more intelligent as well as faster and stronger than you've ever been in the whole of your life. You would be able to fight to protect yourself should the need arise. You would be the best version of yourself that there could ever be."

"And as the years pass, your strength of mind and body would only increase," Lucius added.

Petra expected another long silence, more musing and questioning, but the girl looked up at them both, her eyes intent.

"I wish to become an immortal."

"You are certain? Once you decide, once you are turned, you can never go back to mortality. At that point, you'll have two choices: live forever or die forever."

"I understand. And I want this. I want all that such a life entails."

"You would leave your family behind with no regrets?"

"I will have regrets, but I know if my uncle knew of this, he would wish me to go and never look back. As for my family—my mother and father—they will have one fewer burdensome girl to care for."

"Then you have made your decision, Adélaïs?" Lucius said.

"Yes, Monsieur, I have."

"Then come with us and leave the world as you know it behind."

"We will be your new family," Petra said, pulling Adélaïs into an embrace, feeling as if she were adopting a daughter. And perhaps she was.

"I like how that sounds," Adélaïs whispered, rising from the fountain's edge to take hold of Lucius's outstretched arm.

As they made their way out to their waiting horses, Petra glanced back at the Palais des Papes, now almost wholly mired in the eerie fog.

Forgive us, Monsieur de Chauliac... I promise I will care for your darling girl. Always...

V

The Novitiates

Genoa

August 13, 1345

"**M**ADAME?" ADÉLAÏS WHISPERED, ENTERING THE STUDY WHERE PETRA was writing out a new account for the Immortal Codex. Her servant Dimia had already dressed them both for tonight's rituals. Since Adélaïs would be the first female she would ever turn, she decided to have her dressed in a form-fitted white chemise with a subtle red dagging at the sleeves and a golden girdle with ruby accents at her waist. For reasons of practicality, an overdress and long sleeves would be cumbersome when they entered the ritual pool during the Vellessentia.

The Essentiae and Sanguinea eternae would both have elements of symbolic red in their costumes, a stark reminder of Petra's blood sacrifice for each of them. For herself, she reserved a finer dress of shimmering forest green and gold silk brocade with a massive ankh made of soft gold looped around her neck alongside her ever-present phial of mortanine, a far more expensive bottle than the first she had had in Tibur, Italy back in the old days.

Dimia had parted her hair into elaborate loose braids on either side, complete with spirals of mortanine leaves woven throughout. The final touch was a gold and ruby circlet made of ankhs around the crown of her head.

105

She and Adélaïs had already started work on developing a system for encrypting her daily musings during the month they had been back home in Genoa. The girl had a great deal of work ahead of her, given the vast library of histories Petra would soon have her working on. Even in such a short time, she knew she had made the right decision to bring Adélaïs with them. The girl's intelligence and skill had already proven to be invaluable.

"Yes?" Petra finally looked up from her work and dropped her quill into the rapidly dwindling ink in the well. She already knew what the girl would say.

"The servant bid me tell you the Sanguinea have arrived." Adélaïs's voice belied her fear.

They would begin the Vellessentia within the hour. The first for Adélaïs as well as Clarius's mysterious novitiate. This would be the first ritual ceremony with two novitiates to be turned. Petra hoped she was up for the challenge. The Vellessentiae were always a difficult time of year for her, but those with a novitiate turning weakened her the most. It would take days for her to recover.

Petra worried, too, that Adélaïs's fear of death would make her refuse immortality in the end. It wasn't every day a girl knew the exact hour she would take her last breath. It had been a great many years since Petra had witnessed Nicon, the second Sanguine she had turned, dying from mortanine poisoning. Even for someone like her, who died every year without fail, it was still difficult to watch.

"How many have come?"

"Caelia said there are four, Madame Petra."

"Good." Clarius, thankfully, had not added more novitiates without telling her. "Have you seen our guests yet?"

"No, Madame."

"Remember not to be alarmed by their appearance. They will have silver eyes and dark veins now that my blood is ebbing from their bodies. Yet, don't forget they are all dangerous in their own way. They answer to Clarius, and he is and always will be volatile—especially now that he and Lucius will see each other for the first time in a millennium. Steer clear of the Sanguinea as best you can tonight."

The girl nodded, attempting a brave smile.

"Bid Dimia to request Clarius remain outside and have Guistino escort the rest into the dining room. Remind them not to return to the main house until midday tomorrow."

"Yes, Madame." The girl moved to shut the door behind her.

"Adélaïs? Where is Lucius?"

"I believe he is outside in his workshop."

"Fetch him for me, would you? Tell him our guests are in the dining room taking refreshments. I will be along shortly."

Adélaïs nodded obediently and left the room. Taking a deep breath, Petra slipped outside into the yellow-orange light of a stunning sunset and strode immediately to the main portal of their sprawling palazzo, where three massive arches led out into a central stone courtyard filled with their vegetable and flower gardens. Clarius was leaning against one of the arches, gazing out at the riot of colors over the vineyards far beyond the palazzo.

She gazed for a moment at his profile. The tell-tale dark veins creeping across his jawline spoke of his blood-need, though the fading day hid his ashen skin under a tint of sunset-gold. Still, he was undeniably handsome, his Roman nose as straight as an arrow, his muscles taut beneath the expensive fabrics. But she knew the man beneath that god-like facade. She knew his darkness and his destructive desire.

"Lucius will be joining us this evening, Clarius."

He did not turn at the sound of her voice. He knew she had been standing there. Given his lust for blood, he had a far keener sense of smell than any of them. He had honed his senses over millennia, as a wolf ever gaining skill in the hunt.

"After centuries of cowardice, now he comes?" Clarius had always thought him weak and never hesitated to tell her so. Usually she ignored him, but tonight it grated on her. No matter how much she warned him not to, she knew Clarius would test Lucius's patience tonight. Of that she was certain. What she didn't know was how Lucius would respond. She couldn't deny he had a temper of his own where Clarius was concerned, which was why she hadn't pressed him to attend another Vellessentia until this year. Yet, other than with her, Lucius wasn't used to bowing to anyone—much less to Clarius, a man he would never forgive for murdering his father. Immortality bestowed many gifts; a fading memory of past wrongs was not one of them.

"Because I will be turning a novitiate of my own tonight," she finally said after a prolonged silence. It certainly wasn't her only reason, but the less Clarius knew of the doings of the Essentiae, the safer they would ultimately be.

Clarius glanced back at hearing this.

"Again, why now?"

"What the Essentiae choose to do or not do is none of your concern."

"The hellfire it isn't." His words were laced with growing irritation and suspicion. "You hold my life in your blood, woman."

She sighed as she walked up to stand next to him.

"The novitiate is to be my scribe. She has skill in such things."

Clarius laughed. "You are a fool. After all this time, the first immortal you turn is a girl to write your letters for you?"

He laughed again as Petra tried not to smile and give the secret away. *Oh, my dear Clarius, if only you knew the plans I have for her…*

"It's about time I had a servant I can trust. Though, over time, I know Adélaïs will learn far more. She is quite gifted with words."

"As long as she isn't a threat to my Sanguinea, feel free to people your Essentiae with scribes and poets and fools." He kicked at the stone column he held to and looked out again at the vineyards beyond their sprawling villa.

"I shall do what I wish for my own eternae. And, Clarius"—she turned to look him in the eyes—"you will not talk to her, touch her, or look at her." Petra hoped her voice would convey the threat she meant to send.

Clarius eyed her in amusement. "Considering she'll have to get to know me at some point during our eternity together, why not start out as intimate relations? We are all family, are we not?"

His slow curving smile turned Petra's stomach.

"Adélaïs is younger than I was back in our ancient days. She is afraid. She is far from home. You will do nothing to jeopardize her turning."

"Yes, yes. Have your little servant girl." He turned toward her but kept his arms crossed. "I have much more delicious game to hunt tonight."

"You leave Lucius be. You will not start a war here in my house. I forbid it. Cross me, and I will not turn your novitiate."

"Oh, you will, Petra. The beautiful novitiate Ximena is my new prey. And you know better than to stand between me and my quarry."

"Only a fool would think a woman is such a thing."

"My dear Petra, you are innocent of the ways of men, it seems. Have no fear. You have plenty of time for the learning as do I for the teaching."

He pulled her to him, then, bringing her mouth to his in a kiss. She let him, hoping it would placate him and make him think he had won the battle. He did not yet know her aim was to win the war.

Clarius's kiss was surprisingly sweet. He had bathed his mouth in honey-wine and basil. Had he known he would steal a kiss from her to-night? She did not hold him in the same way he held to her, and she was thankful Lucius was not here to see her growing response to Clarius. His large, cool hands curved around her lower waist possessively, and she felt again the power in his body, felt herself falling into the beginnings of a draw.

His body stiffened, as he sensed the change instinctively. "Ah, not yet, my sweet. I want Lucius to watch as I take you slowly. I want him to remember the first time."

"You bastard." Petra jerked away, letting him see her wipe her mouth of him, and then she turned to walk inside without a word. In a darkened side hallway she stood against a wall, calming her breathing and chiding herself for returning Clarius's kiss with Lucius so close by. She didn't want to do anything to jeopardize this night's Vellessentia. As Clarius passed her on his way into the dining room, she shrank back into the shadows, though he knew she was there.

She needed to get herself together. Keeping the peace between the expanding eternae rested upon her shoulders alone. She had to keep them all from each other's throats, or this night would end in violence. Petra straightened her back and smoothed back her hair. She would get through this, if only for Lucius and for Adélaïs's sake.

When she entered the cavernous dining hall, she gazed at all assembled. It was Lucius's absence she noticed first. Adélaïs had already entered. She sat shyly away from the others at one end of the long, wooden dining table while Clarius and Silvio gulped their wine at the other end. Nicon, a Sanguine she had turned thirty years ago, was talking quietly with who Petra could only assume was Clarius's novitiate. A single glance at the sensual beauty told Petra the woman hailed from Spain, given her manner of dress. She wore a midnight blue velvet overdress with red accents at the elbows and neckline along with a gold and white underdress with fitted sleeves. Her hair was held up in an elaborate *caul* on either side of her head with an attached circlet made of gold and sapphires. Clarius had obviously spared no expense.

The novitiate's unyielding gaze burned cold despite the fact that she was looking at the embodiment of her chance at immortality. Petra could only imagine what lies Clarius had spun in the woman's ear about her.

Nicon pressed a hand to the hilt of his ancient katana sword and bowed in deference to Petra when he noticed her arrival. Petra bowed in return. Of all the Sanguinea, Nicon had been the most respectful to her over the years. She rather liked him. He had once been a celebrated Samurai in the Kamakura shogunate when his name was still Daiki and he lived in Japan.

"Ah, my immortal mother," Clarius called out, raising his glass to her and forcing Silvio to do the same, which ended up with Silvio spilling his wine all over the floor.

"Clarius." Petra inclined her head but gave him no further deference as she swept into the room, her Vellessentiae gown and short train settling around her. "Why don't you introduce me to your novitiate."

"This is Ximena from Valencia, Spain."

"My lady," Ximena said, her voice strong and her gaze piercing. "I was named for the famed wife of El Cid who ruled Valencia after his death."

"The military leader who originally fought for King Ferdinand in Castile?" Petra asked, remembering that period in the 11th century. To this day, he remained one of the most famous Spaniards who ever lived.

The woman nodded proudly.

"Welcome, Ximena. Has Clarius made you aware of what will happen here tonight?"

Clarius scoffed at that.

"I have explained all to my lady Ximena, Prima Vita," Nicon said with a stiff bow.

Petra smiled in acknowledgment. "Thank you, Nicon. Mademoiselle Adélaïs here hails from Avignon, France." Petra waved her over, and the girl moved to stand beside her. "She is niece to the pope's private physician."

Clarius glanced up. "Did you meet the pope, girl?"

"Yes, Monsieur. On many occasions."

"Is he as decadent and foolish as they say?" he asked, laughing at her shocked expression.

"I don't—I mean, that is to say…"

The girl's voice shook with fear, but Petra took her hand in hers and pressed her forward. "Adélaïs is to be my right hand in all things. Clarius, what skills does Ximena bring to the Sanguinea?"

Ximena stepped forward and answered for him. "I am accomplished in deciphering the ancient texts of my people."

Something about the way she said it made Petra wonder if she wasn't being entirely forthcoming about her skill set. It would be just like Clarius to tell one of his Sanguinea not to reveal too much to her. She would have to keep an eye on Ximena.

"You will speak when I say you can speak, woman," Clarius said gruffly.

"You do not know the extent of my knowledge, Clarius," Ximena said defiantly.

He scoffed at her. "And you do not know your place here."

Petra thought this woman too proud, but she had learned to play the game to get along in a world ruled by men. Ximena would find this still true in the Sanguinea eternae, where Clarius was master of all. She would, however, see glimpses of the rule of women with Petra's Essentiae. She wondered if the woman would eventually feel caught between the two eternae and want to defect from the Sanguinea at some point. Time alone would tell. It struck Petra that crossing this woman would unleash a tigress, but she would not be cowed by a novitiate too arrogant to be humbled by the prospect of immortality.

Petra gazed impassively at the woman for a long uncomfortable moment. "Know this, Ximena: on this night, I will become your mother, your source of life, your *Prima Sanguis*. If I cease to exist, you will die. You are here solely at my pleasure"—Petra locked eyes with Clarius—"and I am the one who will decide tonight if you may pass into immortality. You would do well to remember this." Her warning was as much for Clarius's sake as Ximena's.

The woman looked to Clarius for guidance on how to respond, but he and Petra were playing war games with their eyes. It was obvious to Petra that he was struggling not to fly into a rage, but in the end, Lucius saved him the trouble. He flung open the double doors and strode into the room with a vengeance.

He wore a favorite of hers, his mink brown doublet with red velvet siding, which always brought out the rich, deep browns of his eyes. Petra half-expected him to be wearing a sword at his hip, but he only reached out to her, encircling her with his arm possessively, which suited her fine. She leaned up to kiss him, and his immediate response was to draw her more deeply into his mouth. She welcomed it, wanting to repair the damage of their earlier fight. When he pulled away, he gazed into her eyes with a strange look. She worried he smelled Clarius on her, or tasted the basil and honey yet left on her tongue. If he suspected it, he said nothing, but nodded at the others in turn and spared a singular smile for Adélaïs, who tried to smile back through her nervousness.

"Ximena and Nicon," Petra said, walking forward with Lucius, "allow me to introduce our other Essentiae, Lucius." It seemed strange to her even now that Nicon and Lucius had never met.

Lucius's greeting was forced and Ximena's curtsey short, but Nicon's smile and bow were genuine, at least.

"Petra has told me much about you, Lucius. It is an honor to finally make your acquaintance."

"I have heard similarly about you, Nicon. You are most welcome in our home. And, you, Silvio," Lucius asked, raising his chin in a cool greeting, "how fare you?"

"I am well, Luc—" Silvio stopped himself before he made the mistake of calling Lucius by his former slave name. "Lucius, I mean."

Lucius shook his head to dismiss the gaff and walked further into the room. When he finally laid eyes on Clarius, the smug grin on his enemy's face was enough to wipe the pleasant smile from his own.

"So, Lucius, you come at long last to witness a Vellessentia. Why now?"

"In honor of our new Essentia, Adélaïs, Clarius. No more, no less."

"I see you have not changed."

"No more than you. Still the man you always were." They all knew what Lucius meant, that he believed Clarius could never change, no matter how much Petra's blood had quelled him over the centuries.

"I am far more as you will see tonight when I bathe in your lover's blood."

"You will treat her with the honor she deserves, Clarius, or I will have your head."

"Are you really such a monumental fool, Lucius? What do you think we've been doing all these years? This was always a bloody business, no matter how many pretty rituals you surround it with. I take Petra's life at every Vellessentia, a penance she will owe me for an eternity."

"And what price do you pay for her losses, you bastard?" Lucius's voice rose with the color of his face.

"Oh, I've paid the blood price, Lucipor, with every murder I've committed and every drop of blood I've spilled." Clarius was deliberately provoking him with his old slave name now. "I lay all of this at your feet, Mother Petra. A testament to your gift of immortality. A mountain of dead, bloodied and cleaved."

Petra watched in horror as Lucius lurched forward, white-hot rage flashing in his eyes.

VI

The Aeternitescentia

August 13, 1345

IN THE SPACE OF A SINGLE MOMENT, LUCIUS TOOK CLARIUS BY THE THROAT, Nicon drew his sword, and Petra pulled Lucius's mind into an Essentian draw. Clarius raised his fist to strike, but Petra's sudden draw reduced Lucius's strength so fast he let go of Clarius's neck and fell to his knees.

"Pull Clarius back," Petra commanded Nicon.

She knew Nicon saw she was attempting to break the two men up, and he moved to yank Clarius back with both hands, his sword clattering loudly onto the marble floor in the process.

Petra moved around to face Lucius as he gasped and tried to pry her fingers from his head. But she held on harder, drawing his strength and probing deep within his mind. Whether memory or wish, she did not know, but what she saw took her breath away. Petra witnessed Lucius drawing from the heart of a stranger in a darkened alleyway with a full moon high overhead. It was a man, afraid for his life, screaming from the pain and the fear. It was over in a moment's time, and Lucius left him for dead in a pile of refuse, running through the night, away from what he had done, away from the pleasure and the guilt and the power of the draw.

"Let go, Petra." Lucius's voice was hard as steel, and in his eyes, she watched his anger shift from Clarius to her. Then his thoughts exploded into her mind. She saw his desire. To kill... *to kill her*. And hate... Oh, goddess. The hate he felt for her in this moment made her fall to her knees

113

before him. Who was this man he killed? Was she glimpsing a true memory?

"Don't make me do this to you," she whispered. "I will release you, but you must promise me you will not lay a hand on Clarius again. If you do…" She shook her head, wishing she didn't have to say the words. "I will have to punish you under eternae law—our law." She begged him with her eyes not to force her hand. Never once in their history had anyone invoked the vindicatio, a ritual that was both trial and punishment for transgressions against other eternae. But Clarius was now well within his rights to call for one.

When Lucius looked up at her as the pain of her draw shook through him, she withdrew. The abject misery he felt at her chastisement was spreading through his eyes and falling through his thoughts. His rage was gone in an instant, replaced by a deadness, a defeat she hadn't seen since the first time Clarius had forced Lucius to watch as he took her life. A great pain struck her in the chest, and she wanted only to bow before him and beg his forgiveness, but she could not. She had to remain strong in order to keep the appearance of her power. This alone kept Clarius and his Sanguinea from killing Lucius and imprisoning her. Petra glanced over at Adélaïs who looked on from the corner where she cowered with horror. Petra gave her a reassuring smile, but she knew it fell horribly flat.

"Lucius," she whispered, leaning down to him, "Adélaïs is terrified. You do not want her to see you spill blood in anger tonight. Fix your thoughts on her, my love. Do not let your need for vengeance put her in danger."

Lucius searched Petra's face, seeming to seek an answer to the unspoken question in his eyes. He sought her love, and she answered with a soft gaze and an outstretched hand. When he took it and glanced at Adélaïs, Petra realized she had finally gotten through to him. As they rose together, Petra looked at the Sanguinea each in turn.

"We have two novitiates with us tonight who are unaware of our past grievances. It is best we do not frighten them, or they may not wish to join us." She took a moment to glance over at Ximena, who stood by Nicon with anger flashing in her eyes. Clarius, on the other hand, was pretending to be relaxed and bored as he sipped more wine and looked innocently at Petra. "That goes for you too, Clarius."

Clarius gave her a cool smile. "I'm not the one with a temper this evening."

"Silence!" she shouted, shooting him a glare that would have made the old gods quiver. "It is late. Time for us to begin the Vellessentia."

As she said the words, she noticed the sun's light through the open window had long since faded, replaced by an indigo sky filled with ominous clouds. Petra turned and reached for Adélaïs to take hold of her hand. Together the two of them led the way outside into the garden. The silence of the others behind them told Petra she had won the battle. But would she win the final war tonight?

"Ximena and Adélaïs, come forward," Petra said, when they had reached the large courtyard where they would hold the rituals. The servants had long since lit the torches, giving the entire courtyard a warm glow. The eternae stood waiting outside the inner cella and its accompanying pool of water. "Novitiates, each of you will take a torch and walk on opposite sides of the pool."

Petra turned to the group, even though she was unable to look Lucius in the eyes as he stared hard at her. "Now to the cella. Let us begin our eternae rituals." She followed behind them all as each took a torch and silently marched to the cella, the inner sanctum of their ceremonial grounds. Many of the rituals she had cultivated over the years were a culmination of Roman, Greek, and Christian elements. Such was the result of living for centuries in countries far and wide among cultures she both loved and loathed.

Many of the mosaics upon which they walked were of the Greek and Roman gods of her youth. If she couldn't forget those days, she didn't want Lucius or Clarius to forget them either. She risked a glance toward her lover. His eyes, dark and shadowed against the flickering torch lights, were watching her. Hating her? Petra knew he felt she had betrayed him. She knew because she believed it too. Couldn't he see she was protecting him—protecting all of them? Would she believe this if their roles were reversed?

She put her feelings aside and attempted to mentally prepare for tonight's rituals as she picked up the ceremonial *artavus* and the small, shallow amphora that would hold her blood.

She had just about made it to a place of calm when a gentle tug at her sleeve came from Adélaïs.

"Madame Petra? I'm afraid."

"I know. I am sorry we frightened you. Our quarrels go back millennia, and I confess we are not used to having guests."

"What if my courage fails?"

"It is death you fear. But this is only one death, one single mortal death. Your turning will be first. You will see nothing else of tonight's rituals, and when you wake, my brave girl, you will be awake for all time. So focus on me, and I will guide you through."

"Yes, Prima Vita. I will try."

"Now take your torch in hand and let's begin."

Once they had all lined up, Ximena and Adélaïs began their silent march toward the cella. They moved toward opposite sides of the pool, which shimmered in the moonlight, casting glimmers onto their faces. Petra loved this moment of the ritual, when all was reverent and quiet—even Clarius—and the pain had not yet begun. The cella was a sacred place for her, no matter what village or country they lived in. Here she had died and been reborn countless times. It was a symbol of renewal, of immortality, and a testament to their extraordinary lives. And, tonight, she would turn two more souls. She envied them their innocence, their newness. How would immortality change them? Would it make them cruel? Would the endless days fill them with despair? Would they change the world for good or ill?

When each eternae stood below a lit torch attached to the columns surrounding the pool, the novitiates made their way back to face Petra, Adélaïs with a look of fear and Ximena with a look of defiance. Petra drew nearer to the novitiates.

"We are gathered here at our thirteen hundredth and forty-third Vellessentia with two novitiates who await their first turning, their first Aeternitescentia. We welcome you both, Adélaïs and Ximena. We also welcome Lucius, my fellow Essentia who is joining us for the first time. You honor us—and most especially me—with your presence here tonight." She bowed her head to him, hoping he felt the sincerity of her words.

"Adélaïs and Ximena, at this ritual, you must choose which eternae you wish to join: the Essentiae or Sanguinea. No one can make this choice for you, but you must abide by the current and future laws of the eternae you choose.

"First I will speak the laws. First Law: you must not reveal the existence of the Essentiae or Sanguinea to any human without the consent of your eternae's leader. Second Law: It is forbidden to turn a novitiate without consent. Third Law: It is forbidden for any immortal to force a novitiate to choose an eternae. Fourth Law: It is forbidden for an Essentiae and Sanguinea to draw from each other. Fifth Law: It is forbidden to kill another Sanguinea or Essentiae without consent of the leader of your eternae. Sixth Law: If you break any of these laws, all will gather at the next Vellessentia to decide your fate in a Vindicatio Ritual. Do you understand these laws as I have spoken them?"

"Yes," the women said in unison.

"Do you agree to abide by these laws for as long as you live?"

Once again, the women spoke together. "I do."

"Then enter the pool and take your places next to the *Altarae*

Aevitatis." She waved them down toward the center of the pool where the three shallowly submerged, wide stone altars lay. In front of these stood a taller altar where the ritual amphora and artavus were already laid out. As the novitiates descended into the water, Petra picked up the ritual objects from the table and entered the warm water herself, moving to stand before the altar. She addressed Adélaïs first.

"Adélaïs, do you understand that the Aeternitescentia is irreversible? Once the change takes place, you will never be mortal again."

"Yes, Madame."

"Do you understand that once you drink from the phial of mortanine, you must either become one of us or you will die permanently?"

"Yes, Madame."

"Do you wish to choose the Sanguinea or Essentiae eternae, Adélaïs?"

"I choose Essentiae."

Petra smiled at her, and she was pleased to see the girl smile back despite her fear.

"Tonight and henceforth, you will be known among us as Aurelia Deville, our golden one of the city."

She smiled brightly at this. "Thank you, Madame."

"Ascend the altar, Aurelia, and make ready."

The girl walked up the two steps in front of the altar and lay upon it as water dripped from her partially soaked dress. Ximena watched with cool fascination.

Petra held up the artavus. "I give you my blood freely so that you may have a life without end. So long as you abide by our laws, I will never refuse you my lifeblood." She winced as she cut her wrist deeply, knowing she would have need of a full supply before the end. All watched as it spilled into the amphora, rich and dark and full of a life none of them truly understood.

Aurelia shook upon her altar, and Petra didn't know if it was from cold or fear. When enough blood had been spilled, Petra wrapped her wrist in the white cloth that had been set out on the altar and brought the amphora to Aurelia, who took hold of it, though her hands could barely grasp it.

"Have courage," Petra whispered to her. "It's almost over." She knew from her research that the order of elements did not matter, as long as the poison was ingested before a human's death. So to save Aurelia from pain, she had decided to give her the blood and poison at nearly the same time. And the draw would follow close behind.

Aurelia nodded as Petra helped her rise enough to drink from the amphora. She shuddered at the taste, which Petra well knew to be sickly-sweet and metallic.

When she had consumed all of it, Petra set it aside and pulled the stopper from the phial of mortanine.

"This is the final element, Aurelia. Drink this, and you will never die again. Are you ready?"

Aurelia bit her lip. "It will hurt?"

"Yes, it will hurt at first, but I will hasten you with a draw of your mind. When you are near death, the draw will begin to soften the pain into a kind of ecstasy. At the moment of your death, you will feel no more pain."

Aurelia nodded, unable to say more. Petra lifted the phial to her lips and poured it into the girl's mouth, regretting the pain it would soon cause.

"I will begin the draw now. Cling to me and don't let go." Petra took a strong hold of her head and dug in, drawing as fast as she ever had in her life, nothing in her mind now but the thought of quickening the girl's death.

When Aurelia's jaw went slack and her arms limp, Petra began to see the girl's thoughts emerge. Strange numbers and letters appeared—ciphers perhaps?—and then faces materialized in the darkness. Petra didn't recognize any of them as they looked down upon her, shouting and ridiculing. Then there was Guy de Chauliac himself, pulling her away from what appeared to be her family, comforting her. He brought her another cipher to figure out, and then another, always smiling, always laughing. "I love you, Uncle. You'll never leave me, will you?"

"No, my dear girl, but you will…"

And then she was gone. Aurelia fell limp against Petra's arms, her eyes closed in peaceful repose. Petra curled her into an embrace, wishing she could have given her a more painless end.

"I'm so sorry, sweet girl," she whispered. "Forgive me this one transgression. Let go of the life I take and embrace the immortal you will become."

It seemed the entire night had fallen silent at the moment of her passing. When Petra finally laid her down to rest against the hard stone of the altar, she wiped tears away and looked up at Lucius, the only one who could possibly understand her sadness. And he did. She saw it in the slump of his shoulders, in his unwavering stare.

Petra sighed and turned to Ximena, whose former coldness had been wiped away in the face of Aurelia's death. She stood as stone-like as the altar she hid behind.

"Ximena, I chose Aurelia to turn first because she was so young and frightened. But now I come to you with the same questions. Do you understand the Aeternitescentia is irreversible?"

"Yes." Ximena's voice faltered, but she steeled her gaze and summoned up her courage.

"Once the mortanine is administered, you must either become one of us or you will die permanently. Do you acknowledge and understand this?"

"Yes." Her voice was stronger now.

"Do you wish to choose the Sanguinea or Essentiae eternae, Ximena?"

Ximena glanced up at Clarius, who nodded.

"Sanguinea," he burst out, his tone impatient and commanding.

"Hold, Clarius." Petra held up her hand to him. "You know the law. You will not speak for this woman. She must choose of her own free will."

"I choose Sanguinea," she said, her voice once again filled with the same coldness as before.

"Ximena, the name I choose for you is Phaedra, which means bright in the ancient language of my youth. And since the sigil of your namesake's esteemed husband is marked by lions, your surname shall be de Leon."

Petra expected resistance, but the woman seemed pleased, even inclining her head in acknowledgment. It occurred to Petra, then, that this woman had as changeable a personality as Clarius. She wondered if this was why he had chosen her, because he recognized himself in her. Whatever the reason, it did not bode well for the Essentiae. The last thing her eternae needed was a volatile, headstrong woman coming between them and Clarius. Petra had enough trouble quelling his bloodlust year after year.

For a moment, Petra considered rejecting his novitiate, but she knew it would end in a bloodbath and threaten the balance of power between the two eternae. No, she must be patient and plan carefully. She could never be rash or foolish. His bloodlust made him more powerful every passing century. He could not be killed with cunning or strength alone. It would have to be a full-on assault and the most intelligent strategy they could devise. For that she needed a small army, one she would carefully build over centuries.

"Clarius, approach the Altar Aevitatus. It is time for your novitiate's Aeternitescentia."

They had discovered centuries ago that to turn a true Sanguinea, she had to let Clarius drink from the novitiate during the Aeternitescentia Ritual. They had yet to learn why this was so, but Petra hoped to find out more as advances were made in science. She suspected it was the violence of the kill but had no direct evidence to support her theory.

While Clarius always had difficulty keeping his bloodlust under control during the rituals, Petra saw immediately that tonight was different. Clarius leapt into the pool, splashing water all over the prone body of Aurelia, his silver eyes flashing with need. Lucius stepped forward, awaiting Petra's command to strike. She waved him off and pushed against Clarius's chest as Phaedra moved to the opposite side of her altar to put distance between her and Clarius.

"Stand back, Clarius! I must give her the mortanine first. Unless you wish her to die permanently?"

"Hurry up, woman. The blood… her blood, it calls to me."

Petra rather wanted him to suffer, but she did not wish the same for Phaedra. She might not trust the woman, but she didn't hate her as she hated Clarius.

"Lay upon the altar, Phaedra, while I prepare my blood for you."

Clarius himself pulled Phaedra up into his arms and laid her on the Altar Aevitatus. He was rough with her, but she did not cry out. As Petra removed the cloth from her wrist and sliced more deeply this time, Clarius loomed over Phaedra, licking his lips as he pressed her arms down.

"Soon you'll be one of us, but now it's time for my first taste of you," he said, his smile ghoulish in the flickering torch lights.

Petra was grateful, at least, Aurelia was not alive to see what Clarius would do to Phaedra. She would learn soon enough just how hideous he could be, but she wanted to shield the girl as much as she could on this night.

Once Petra had spilled enough blood into the amphora, she set the ritual objects aside and let her blood freely flow from her wrist. It no longer mattered. Soon she would be dead alongside Phaedra, Aurelia, and Clarius.

She brought the amphora to Phaedra, careful to stand on the opposite side of the Altar Aevitatus from Clarius. She caught his gaze, surprised to see him looking at her when he had been so fixated on the object of his prey. The look in his eyes told her he was remembering their kiss, that he was really waiting for her blood—not Phaedra's. She looked down at the woman, who was shivering with the fear she should have felt all along.

"Phaedra, I give you my blood freely so you may have a life without end. So long as you abide by our laws, I will never refuse you my lifeblood. Clarius, lift her up so she may drink."

He curled his arm around her back to lift her up as Petra administered the blood herself. Phaedra's hands were shaking too much to hold the amphora. She began to spit it up, but Petra held to her shoulder and gave her an encouraging smile.

"Slowly, Phaedra. You must drink it all. This is the taste of immortality. Bitter, yes, but sweet in its way."

This seemed to calm Phaedra. She focused her hard gaze on Petra, as if begging her for help.

Oh, no, my dear. Nothing and no one can save you from him now…

Petra glanced up at Lucius, then. Going through the Vellessentia with him for the first time in centuries upon centuries filled her with a strange mix of anger and guilt and desire. She felt his love and his jealousy like a palpable current moving through the air. This both pleased and horrified her, and when she realized Phaedra had finished drinking, Petra couldn't bear to feel his eyes on her any longer.

"I will give you mortanine, Phaedra, which will complete the process. Then Clarius will…" Petra glanced up at him, not wanting to frighten the woman further but not finding any comforting words to lessen the horror.

"Finish you off," Clarius said, his smile only reaching one side of his face as it curled up in pleasure at Phaedra's obvious terror.

"Clarius, please," Petra admonished. He wasn't listening. He was back to staring at his novitiate's neck.

"Come, Phaedra, drink," Petra said, tipping the poison into her mouth as she sputtered and coughed, blood staining her lips. "Now, Clarius, ease her suffering instead of sating your lust."

It took only a moment before he was tearing at the woman's neck, her screams mixing with the sounds of his lips sucking from her neck. Blood stained her beautiful skin and gown, and she reached out for Petra.

"Try to relax. The pleasure of the draw will come soon, Phaedra." Petra regretted her words, knowing they reminded Lucius that the Sanguine draw provoked as much pleasure in her as it did pain. And there, Petra saw it in Phaedra's eyes. The desire for more washed over her features as she descended swiftly into death. When the time came for her own turn at Clarius's mouth, would she be able to hide that moment of rapture from Lucius?

When Phaedra's eyes closed for the last time, Clarius turned to Petra. "I've had better," he said, wiping the dark blood dripping from his teeth and lips. "And she'll soon be mine for the taking."

VII

The Leave-taking

August 13, 1345

"CLARIUS, YOU WILL RELEASE YOUR NOVITIATE AND STEP AWAY FROM THE altar." Petra said, attempting to keep her tone level as she felt Lucius's eyes on her. She sensed his anger growing like a storm, threatening to touch down at any moment. "Essentiae and Sanguinea, we will now begin the Renascentia Ritual."

Petra took the amphora and artavus and brought them to the altar while Clarius vaulted onto the central altar. This time Petra dug deeper with the blade, the pain intensifying as the blood poured from her veins. She felt herself weakening, and it scared her this time. For how would she protect Lucius if she died too soon?

When she had bled enough, she took up the amphora and ascended the steps out of the pool into the cool night air. She offered her blood first to Silvio.

"I give you my blood freely so you may have a life without end. So long as you abide by our laws, I will never refuse you my lifeblood."

He bowed his head to her and drank until she pulled the amphora away. When she did the same for Nicon, he whispered, "The situation is dangerous. Let me know if you need me."

Petra nodded, grateful he would offer assistance to her even though she was not in his eternae. She worried she would have to take him up on his offer.

When she stood before Lucius, the depth of his agony lay as a raw

123

wound in his eyes. There was no need for words. She had none to give to ease his pain. She wanted to fall inside herself and disappear. She wanted to kill Clarius and end this madness once and for all. But she could not. Lucius had to move past this. He had to be a part of the Vellessentia if they were to survive through the millennia and build their army. No matter how much this grieved him, she had to fight the pull of his anger and bitterness.

"Lucius, I give you my blood freely so you may have a life without end. So long as you abide by our laws, I will never refuse you my life-blood."

Lucius hesitated, and she worried he would refuse her blood. "I don't think I can watch this, Petra. I can't—"

"You must. If you leave now, it will put us all in danger. I would survive, but you and Aurelia would not. I couldn't bear that. Please."

"Never again, Petra. I would rather die."

She squeezed his arm, hoping Clarius wouldn't notice. Even with her blood staining his lips, Lucius looked like a god. She wanted to reach out to him, to wipe away that blood with her fingers, but she dared not. It seemed Lucius wanted to do the same. He reached up to stroke her cheek with his thumb, but she shied away, fearing it would inflame Clarius's anger. Lucius's expression fell and his hand dropped to his side as he looked away from her. She could do nothing more but retreat to the pool and face her executioner with her lover looking on.

She had barely set the amphora on the altar before Clarius was there dragging her toward the Altar Aevitatus, the lust in his eyes reaching its breaking point. She felt the energy and desire coming off his skin in waves. It thrilled and terrified her as always. The terror came from knowing that no matter what happened, she would never escape death from this point on. The desire was the anticipation of the ecstasy she knew was coming. There was no experience in the world like it, not even with Lucius—a fact she hoped to conceal from her lover for an eternity.

"You're mine, Petra. Body, soul, and blood." He had barely pressed her body onto the stone altar before his sharp teeth had penetrated the delicate skin of her throat. She had promised herself she would not cry out no matter how rough he was with her. She would not make it harder for Lucius to endure. So she bit her lip and screamed silently as the pain burned through her body. The blood loss made her woozy.

With a jarring snap, Clarius jerked away from her. In a haze of confusion and growing madness, she shook her head to clear her mind and that's when she heard him speak. He was calling out, his voice echoing across the water and off the stones.

124

"Want a taste, Lucius? A taste of what you can never truly have?" Then Clarius's bloodied lips were on her own, and he was kissing her. She struggled against him, disgusted, terrified, knowing what such a sight would do to Lucius.

She heard her lover's scream. A guttural cry of anguish and burning wrath. Shouts erupted everywhere, and Clarius finally released her from his kiss.

"Stop!" she tried to shout, but it came out too weak to be heard by anyone. She tried again. "Nicon, keep Silvio back. Lucius, don't come near us."

He was already in the pool, striding swiftly toward them, the artavus held high in his hand. Clarius shoved her aside and faced Lucius head on.

"No, Lucius, stop!" Petra shouted. "The law forbids you. I forbid you."

He could no longer hear her voice. He saw only his enemy now. Petra fell off the stone and grabbed hold of Clarius's arm, pulling herself along with him through the water.

Petra put herself between them at the last moment, hoping it would stop Lucius from doing the unthinkable. But he had already thrust the dagger forward, and she felt it dive deep into her abdomen. A scream rent the night air, and it wasn't until she saw Lucius's horrified face that she realized the cry had come from her.

"No…" Lucius whispered, his mouth agape with shame and dread. The artavus fell from his hand, and she tried to focus her mind away from the pain but found she could not. It took her breath away.

"Thought you'd finish her off first, did you?" she heard Clarius say as if through a dream.

Lucius seemed not to hear him as he stared at her without moving.

She closed her eyes, bit her lip, tried not to cry as she realized there was only one thing that would force him to leave. *Yes, say it. Spurn him to save him.* "Go, Lucius. I don't want you here. I don't want you anymore."

He brought the back of his hand up to his mouth, as if to silence all he wanted to say—or perhaps, all he could not say.

"Petra…" he whispered, and then he backed away, shaking his head, his eyes dark with despair.

She watched him as he moved away from her, every step a dagger, only this time to her heart. When he finally turned toward their fields and his shadowy body disappeared into the darkness, she let her tears flow unchecked down her cheeks.

"Draw me, woman!" Clarius shouted in her ear.

"I'm too weak," she whispered, as she clutched at her stomach, the blood from her wound staining the water around them, her legs failing her. "Lift me up to the altar, Clarius. Do it now." The shooting pains in her wound felt like she was being stabbed over and over. To her surprise, he did as she asked and laid her atop the hard stone.

"My strength is gone, Clarius. I cannot draw you."

"That bastard will pay for this." He shook her hard. "I'll kill him!"

"Touch him, Clarius, and I will never draw you again."

His stare burned into her, a searing brand of his coming vengeance. "I want you to die slowly, Petra, knowing he was the one who killed you in the end. I will make sure he knows it too."

"You can't do that. You must be quelled. You must drink—"

"No." He pushed her away and scoffed. "This isn't finished. At the next Vellessentia, I will call for a Vindicatio, and I will have his head." With that, he left her, his Sanguinea filing out silently behind him.

Her body grew cold from blood loss and shock. Her energy was spent. She felt the death throes even now. Everything she had feared would happen had come to pass, and now she had lost Lucius. Even if he came back, Clarius would force her to punish him for breaking eternae law. She had been selfish and cruel to make her lover watch. And all because just once… just once she didn't want to die alone surrounded by her enemies.

She closed her eyes to the world and prayed to the old gods to never wake her again.

The Veil of Time

Sicily

February 21, 1723

"CLARIUS IS A MONSTER!" AURELIA EXCLAIMED. "WHY DID YOU NEVER tell me all this?"

"I wanted to keep as much of it from you as I could back then, Aurelia." The Prima Vita's voice was soft, as it had been during the telling, as though to speak in whispers made it more bearable.

"But why? I would have——"

"You might have run away, Aurelia," Lucius interjected, his voice gentle.

"I couldn't have had that," Petra said. "I needed you. We needed you. But I knew then as I know now what it has cost you. I have always been aware of the danger I put you in every time Clarius came to us at Vellessentia. I hoped his fascination with me would never waver or lean toward you."

"And if it had?"

Petra shook her head. "I don't know, Aurelia. He is stronger than all of us. I have only ever had one power over him—a power that is both a weakness and a strength—and that is my Prima Sanguis."

"You forget one more, Madame," Aurelia said, looking from her to Lucius.

127

Petra raised an eyebrow, disbelieving there could ever be anything else.

"The loyalty of those who love you. Lucius. Cassian. Me." Aurelia wondered where Cassian was at this moment. She knew it unlikely he'd be in bed at this hour. Of all the Essentiae immortals, he was the most guarded, the most reclusive. He had always been thus. Cassian often wandered the deserted Sicilian shores late at night—doing what, God only knew.

Petra laughed. "You and Lucius maybe. Cassian… I think not."

It was Aurelia's turn to shake her head. "He loves you, my lady. Even when he doesn't know how to show it."

"You think that if it eases your mind."

Petra smiled graciously at her, but Aurelia was not fooled by her flippant dismissal. She knew as well as the rest of them did that Cassian wouldn't hesitate to lay down his life for her. For any of them.

"Lucius?" Petra asked, a frown creasing her forehead as she leaned toward him. "When I… drew you during the Aeternitescentia, I saw a man in your memories. A man that you killed…"

Lucius shook his head. "That is a story for another time, Petra."

By the way he said it, with a blunt finality in his tone, Aurelia knew he would not speak further about it. For a painful moment, they both watched as the questioning in Petra's gaze dissipated into frustration, but he refused to speak again.

After several moments of silence, Aurelia couldn't bear it anymore. "What happened after you…?" she began.

"Died?" Petra finished, looking grateful that Aurelia had changed the topic, as if she didn't truly want to know Lucius's answer after all. "I awoke to a home that was an empty echo of what it once had been. Lucius was gone by the time I opened my eyes, as you may well remember."

The lady glanced over at him, and the look passing between them brought tears to Aurelia's eyes. Lucius reached up, and with the lightest of touches, trailed a thumb across Petra's cheek. He whispered to her, but Aurelia didn't catch it. A lover's apology, perhaps?

For a moment, they were lost in each other, and Aurelia watched them. She had always thought of them this way. Never each alone but always as part of a whole that could not be if they were not together. And, yet, she had known them to be apart through the years. She had been there to witness Petra's longing when he would go away from her each Vellessentia. To see that pain, to witness it, was agonizing. Aurelia couldn't fathom what it would be to live it—not just once but for ages upon ages. Their greatest beauty was something they would never see. Only those surrounding them could. It was the moment when they were looking at each other, when the world fell away, and they were the only two people on Earth.

Petra shook herself from her lover's gaze and smiled sheepishly at Aurelia. "Where was I?"

"Upon waking after the Vellessentia of 1345…?" Aurelia reminded her.

"Ah, yes. My cries for Lucius woke you that first morning of your immortal life, Aurelia. I know I frightened you, and I am sorry for it."

"I do remember, but I was so young, and my memory will never come close to matching yours."

"Count yourself blessed in that regard, young one." Petra's laugh was soft, and she exchanged a smile of amusement with her lover.

"I certainly do," he said.

"Where did you go, Lucius?" Aurelia asked. "You were gone so long."

He glanced at Petra, then, but did not respond. Yet, the answer was there in the air between them all, thick as it was with the veil of time and sadness.

PART III

1346

Kaffa, Crimea

I

The Search

Genoa

July 28, 1346

PETRA MOVED AS ONE DEAD THROUGH THE MARKETPLACE. GENOA, ITALY was a city-state of bustling markets filled with sea-bass and mackerel strung up in the shops and carts overflowing with various cheeses, shell-fish, honey, and barley grain. Even the famous Genoese lace and blue jean fabrics fluttered in the on-shore breeze of the womens' carts. The scent of freshly dropped donkey manure was the only thing that caught a moment of her attention. She had left Aurelia home on this excursion and took no servants with her. She wanted to disappear in the crowd.

It wasn't wine or bread or jewels from exotic lands she looked for. No, it was Lucius. It was the hopeless hope she might accidentally run into him here. She was desperate to tell him all was forgiven, to ask him if he would ever forgive her. She wanted him to draw from her, to take her into him and dissolve her utterly into his body. He had been gone far too long. Nearly a year and still no word of his whereabouts, despite all the spies she had sent out looking for him.

As long as Petra had known him, he had never revealed where he would go when he left her during the Vellessentiae. She asked him countless times, but he would never say. What worried her most were the rumors of a deadly illness sweeping down Asia and across Rus. Her first

133

thought was to worry Lucius might catch it. Her second thought was the reassurance he was an immortal. Her third thought was that if she had no idea where he was, she wouldn't be able to save him in time if he were dying in some stranger's bed on the far side of the world.

She stopped in the middle of the milling throng and raised her fingers absently to her lips, thinking. How could she get word of him? They had both moved through the world as apparitions, never staying in any one place too long. These days they favored the rich wine country of Genoa though they would soon have to leave again as they had already been here for twenty years. It was far from their old villa they kept in Rome and even Clarius's ancient villa in Tivoli. They knew not a single soul abroad these days. If Lucius died somewhere without her, he would be lost forever.

She shook her head, unable to fully contemplate the thought.

"Ferox, tell Adrianus about the Genoese soldier you met in *Kaffa*, Crimea. You won't believe it," Petra overheard a man say over near the fish stall. "He calls him 'the Immortal.'"

Petra immediately glanced up at the man who spoke. The gruff-voiced, bearded man wore the fine fabrics of a foreign goods trader, complete with a chain of gold around his neck and bags of spices tucked under each arm. Judging by his features and sun-kissed coloring, she knew he must be Genoese, but his accent had the lilt of something foreign in it. Looking more closely at the garb of the three men, she figured they all must be merchants.

"That is what the Kaffans called him. He was more than an ordinary man—that I can tell you."

Petra moved closer, hiding behind the wall of the shop as the men gathered near the displays of shrimp and squid. She wanted to hear every word of the merchant's story. She dared not hope they spoke of Lucius, but she couldn't help herself. She had to know for sure.

Ferox cleared his throat, leaned in, and began his tale. "So, I, too, heard tell of a Genoese who recently sailed to Kaffa on a spice run when I voyaged there late last year. The tales I heard seemed far-fetched, but as I made my way into the city to buy some cumin and coriander, I saw the man myself. I knew he was the Immortal the moment I laid eyes on him."

"Was he a soldier or merchant?" Adrianus, a short, stocky fellow with greying hair, asked Ferox.

"I don't know, but if he wasn't a soldier, he should have been. What an asset to have in war. I would send him to the front lines to lead the charge if I were one of the great generals of Europe."

"Why so?" asked Adrianus.

"I will tell you what I saw, and then you will know," Ferox said. "The citizenry of Kaffa all gathered in the main square to watch him that day."

"Watch him do what?" Adrianus interrupted.

"Wait for it," the third man said, exchanging knowing smiles with Ferox.

"This man was taking beatings by anyone who would come forward. He was stripped to the waist. If you had seen what he looked like… Welts everywhere. Blood pouring from wounds that would have killed any other man. Scars crisscrossing his body. Yet, the man felt no pain."

Petra slapped a hand over her mouth to stop herself from screaming. No, it couldn't be Lucius. He wouldn't… But she had hurt him deeply. She saw it in his face after he stabbed her. And she told him to leave. What had she expected? He was only honoring her request.

"Why? Why would he do such a thing?" Adrianus asked, his voice rising into a higher pitch.

"For money, of course! What else?"

Petra had no idea what to think. Would Lucius be so foolish? So reckless? She had no way of knowing unless she saw this "Immortal" with her own eyes.

She strode over to the men. "Forgive me, Signori, but I overheard your fascinating story. The man you spoke of… is he still in Kaffa, do you think? That is in the Crimea, is it not?"

The men looked her up and down suspiciously. It was not customary for women to approach a group of men in such a way.

Ferox smiled, curiosity and lust alighting his eyes as he looked her up and down. "I believe he is, Signora. Do you know this man?"

"I am not sure. Do you happen to remember the color of his eyes?"

Ferox seemed surprised by the question. "If I recall rightly, he seemed to have strangely colored eyes like yours, but I don't remember the exact color."

Petra silently screamed. It had to be Lucius. The man must have noticed the silver of Lucius's eyes, a clear indicator it was time for him to come home to her.

"Do you know of any ships sailing for Kaffa from the port of Genoa?" she asked Ferox.

"Yes, I'm a sailor aboard the galley *Athena*. We sail with the morning tide."

"I need to book passage."

"You alone?" he asked, obviously scandalized by the notion.

"And one manservant," she quickly added, though she had no intention of bringing anyone.

"Ah. You would need to send your servant to the port and have him ask for Captain Gratian. But the ship is full of cargo, Signora. There is likely no room for passengers."

"I have no doubt the captain will accommodate me, Signore," she replied, and took her leave of the men, who stared after her, mouths agape.

After paying Captain Gratian an exorbitant amount of money, Petra boarded the galley *Athena* alone that night under cover of a hooded cloak. She went straight to her cramped cabin, and there she foolishly let her fears consume her, let her mind go mad with the possibility that Lucius had meant to leave her for all time. She went from berating herself for pushing him away to anger that he would leave her for Clarius to do with as he would. She spent her first sleepless night aboard the *Athena* oscillating between wanting to draw the life out of him and wanting to make love to him.

When the images of Lucius started to surface as her mind drifted into a half-sleep, she let them come, grateful at least for tonight that she had the ability to conjure him up before her in such exquisite detail. She imagined him lying beside her, his warm skin a welcome reprieve from the cold winds outside and the scratch of the woolen blankets surrounding her.

"Lucius," she whispered, "I am coming. Wait for me…"

The following day, the sailor Ferox caught sight of her as she emerged from below deck.

"Signora, you made it aboard."

"As you see." She inclined her head to him. In the shock of morning sunlight, he appeared a little older than she had first thought. Late 20s or early 30s, she figured. He had a handsome face with a strong jaw and warm brown eyes, though his body was thin and wiry.

"Stop your gawking and get back to work, the lot of you," yelled Captain Gratian, a portly man with a shock of white hair and a giant nose.

It was then that Petra noticed they had all stopped to stare at her, even the men hanging from the lines above.

"There is to be no addressing the lady during our sail. If you do, I'll leave you at the next port." All the sailors immediately went back to their work, though they still snuck glances her way. It wasn't every day an average sailor caught sight of an immortal with eyes that could take your breath—and life—away.

"Thank you, Captain Gratian," she said.

He bowed to Petra, obviously taken with her beauty and fine clothes and jewels. She had brought all her most expensive jewelry and finest fabrics, and had her servants sew more jewels and coins into her cloak, as she had no idea what or who she would come across in her travels. Petra wanted to travel light and be ready for any eventuality.

As she moved aft to a far corner of the deck, Petra held up to the light the one thing she was never without: her phial of mortanine. Though she rarely traveled alone without Lucius, the poison was an extra safeguard beyond her own skills. Lucius had also insisted centuries ago that they both learn to defend themselves, so through the years they trained with various sword and bow masters. Petra held her own against Lucius when they trained. He was stronger by far, but she was faster and slightly defter with the blade. These days, she always traveled with the dagger Lucius had given her.

Petra watched the men close-haul the sails and tack against the stiff, warm winds drawing in from the east. It was a magnificent morning, but she took no pleasure in it. Always on her mind was Lucius. She didn't want to admit to herself the real reason for her worry, but she couldn't help the fear that took over, making her clutch the phial of poison more tightly. She feared he was already dead, that he would leave her to this world for an eternity without him.

With her own family dead for millennia, and only servants to punctuate their endless lives, she relied on Lucius most. Yet, now there was Aurelia, which was a comfort. But in the face of Lucius's loss? A shiver ran up her spine, and she pulled her cloak's hood closer around her neck. And Clarius? Clarius who had taken her to heights of madness and anger? Who had stolen her youth, murdered her mother? What was he to her now? A necessary means to an end. A madman she could quell with an ounce of her blood. Her immortal enemy.

She and Lucius had yet to discover the secret of her blood. Without this knowledge, they couldn't hope to extricate themselves from Clarius and his eternae without a bloodbath. She had seen it in Clarius's mind so clearly. And with her *antiqua memoria*, she couldn't forget even if she wanted to. Whenever her mind went back to the thoughts of hatred she had glimpsed in Clarius's mind, she would conjure up Lucius lying beside her, and remember with perfect detail any words of love he had ever said to her. Yet it would only keep her worries at bay for a time, and her dread would come back with a vengeance.

Ferox lumbered down the deck near to her, and after realizing the captain was on the other side of the ship, she got his attention with a smile.

"The man you spoke of yesterday in the market—the man in Kaffa—did anyone mention his name?"

"I heard many names, Signora. Some called him a god. Others called him a saint. Still others named him "the Immortal.""

"No true forename?"

"No, Signora. I heard none spoken." He glanced around beyond her. "No manservant?"

Her smile was stiff. "No, he could not come after all."

For an instant, the man's smile held a hint of lascivious intent.

"Ferox!" Captain Gratian shouted. "Get back to work."

When Ferox glanced back at Petra, his warm smile had returned.

She clutched at the mortanine hanging between her breasts, realizing that she had only one other phial sewed into her cloak. She would have to use it as a last resort. If she killed them all, there would be no one left to sail her across the Sea.

Petra thought again about the Immortal Ferox had spoken of. She was well aware she may be on a fool's errand, yet who else but Clarius and Lucius could take such a beating and survive? If the man had done it for money, then he obviously knew such violence could not ultimately hurt him. But for money? She knew neither Lucius nor Clarius needed it. Both of their eternae, Clarius's growing Sanguinea and her Essentiae, were beyond wealthy, having either worked for or stolen any money or land they needed over the centuries.

Clarius was, of course, reckless enough to do something so foolish. But Lucius? He had a steady mind and heart in all things apart from her.

After an increasingly rough day at sea under heavily reefed sail through a massive storm, she decided to turn in early when the winds finally died down. She had just pushed her stateroom door open when a dirt-caked hand reeking of ale and grease clamped over her mouth. She knew without seeing it was Ferox. He pushed her into the cramped stateroom and slammed the door behind them.

Whenever she found herself in such situations, she had learned long ago that the first step was to stay calm. She would focus inward first, to remind herself of who and what she was. She was immortal. She had died over a thousand times before. She would die again. She would rise again.

Her second task was always to study her surroundings, to look for the nearest escape route or weapon, to decide whether to use guile or violence to achieve her goal.

In the past, she might have used her fighting skill. After all, she had her dagger safely tucked into its strap around her thigh. No, tonight, she would use guile… and poison. Easier to explain away his death.

Ferox shoved her up against the door, his hand still over her mouth. Petra relaxed every muscle in her body and let him feel her smile beneath his fingers. When she motioned with her eyes toward the tiny berth in the corner, surprise lit his eyes. In his confusion, he let his hand slip from her mouth, so she grabbed at the chance.

"There's no need to rush, Ferox. I know what you want, and I want it too."

He was so shocked that he stepped back from her as though she were an apparition. He wouldn't know what she truly was until it was far too late.

She walked further into the cabin to put him more at ease, though he stood in the center of the room, dumbfounded as to how to proceed. She knew just the thing.

"I smuggled a bit of wine aboard, Ferox. Shall I pour you some first?"

"Woman, you surprise me."

"Oh?" She noticed he hadn't used the formal "signora" when addressing her.

"You're not like—like any…"

"Woman you've ever met? No, you're quite right about that. And you'll never meet my equal again. So we'd best make the most of it." She flashed him her most winning smile and turned her back toward him as she rummaged among her things for the small bottle of wine she had brought for Lucius. It was his favorite vintage from their best vineyard. A rich, deep red.

"I've not had a woman in a year," Ferox breathed into her ear. He reached around to grasp at her breasts, and she forced herself not to pull away.

"I can well believe it, seeing as you are a sailor. Sit on the bed, and I will bring you your wine. It's a fine Sangiovese." She held up the bottle for him to view the expensive wine, and his smile of jubilance was genuine.

"What is your name, or shall I call you goddess Aphrodite?"

"Call me whatever you like," she said, as she slipped a healthy pour of mortanine into the bottle. "I will be your salvation tonight, Ferox." She couldn't bear to look at him this time, so she stoppered the bottle and the phial and stood rocking with the ship's movements for a moment, going into the place inside of her where all she could see were Lucius's endlessly brown eyes in her mind's eye.

She lost herself there, for how long she knew not. It was only Ferox's arms coming around her again that brought her out of it. For a moment, she thought about letting him have his way with her so she could pretend his warm body was Lucius's, but when the smell of Ferox's unwashed body hit her again, she remembered herself, and handed him the glass of wine as she removed her over-warm cloak and turned to face him.

She almost felt sorry for the man when he downed a sizable gulp of the fragrant wine. Almost.

"Now, you drink," he said. "It will loosen your tongue and your legs, I promise you." Lust turned his smile into a prurient grin.

"The poison you drank is going to loosen your hold on life, my dear boy," she replied, "but I suppose we all need a little relaxation, no?"

"What—?" Before he even spoke the word, she watched the mortanine taking effect. When his jaw began to seize up, he was smart enough to know she had spoken the truth.

"You whore!" He grabbed her, and before she could react, he tipped the glass over and poured it into her mouth. She immediately spit it out into his face, but too much of it had already slid down her throat, choking her.

Her anger soon matched his own, and she threw the bottle against the far bulkhead, enjoying the shattering sound as she took hold of his head, digging her fingers into his skull as she drew the life from him. Between the mortanine's effects and her Essentian draw, she dispatched him quickly enough.

She had never done a draw while under the thrall of death. It exhausted her strength more quickly than anything else before it. Even with Clarius, his Sanguine draw turned from pain to a euphoric pleasure that drew her into death with a swoon of ecstasy. This was altogether more painful, more draining. And, though she wished for the mortanine to kill her, she did not die right away. Her blood was too powerful now to let her go so easily.

She lay in agony beside the man she had murdered, watching his corpse go through its rigors of death through the night hours. As the moon's light faded into sun, her body gave up its long fight. She had never been more grateful for death, more hopeful for her blood to wash her body and mind clean.

II

The Stone

The Black Sea

August 13, 1346

PETRA AWOKE TO THE BITE OF COLD WIND, THE SCRATCH OF BURLAP AGAINST her bare skin, and the irritating boom of a man calling out.

> "By the power of your Word
> you stilled the chaos of the primeval seas,
> you made the raging waters of the Flood subside,
> and calmed the storm on the sea of Galilee.
> As we commit the earthly remains
> of our brother and sister Ferox Bian-
> chi and Signora Petra to the deep—"

Petra sucked in a breath and sat up. The shouts of sailors erupted all around her. Her eyelids snapped open and through the holes in the burlap sack they had sewn her into, she could see they had gathered to give her and Ferox a burial at sea.

After she had taken a few breaths to calm her own hysteria, she spoke out above the din of shouts and prayers and curses.

"Captain Gratian, if you will be so kind as to release me. As you can see, I am very much alive."

"Signora Petra, is it truly you?" He knelt and ripped open the burlap,

141

letting it fall around her. "I felt for your heart myself. No pulse or breath showed that you survived. Are you mortal or spirit?"

She wanted to say neither. "I am as alive as you are. Help me to my feet, Captain. This chill wind will be the death of me yet."

At this, the men gathered closer around. She glimpsed the horror and fear on their faces, which didn't bode well for the rest of her journey. Sailors were notoriously wary of having women aboard ships.

The captain ripped open the burlap and pulled the rough cloth away from her face, which immediately set her body to shivering. She realized she was dressed only in her chemise. Likely they had stripped her belongings and meant to sell them in Kaffa when they reached the Crimea.

"Your cloak, Captain?" she said, crossing her arms over her exposed skin as the men stood around gawking.

The captain shut his gaping mouth and deftly removed his cloak to cover her. Petra clasped it around her neck and reached up for him to assist her. He hesitated.

"I am flesh and blood, Captain Gratian. Just a little tired from my ordeal."

He took her hand and gently helped her rise, but he released her hand quickly and continued to stare hard at her face. Without breaking eye contact with her, he shouted abruptly to his men. "Stop gawking, or I'll dock your rations!"

"My personal effects, Captain?" she asked.

"If you'll forgive me, Signora... I need to know what happened to Sailor Ferox."

She pulled the cloak further around her, which did nothing to warm her bare feet or help her come up with a good explanation.

"Captain," she began slowly, "as I was retiring after supper last night, Ferox forced himself into my quarters and attempted to rape me."

The captain's eyes widened, but he said nothing.

"The only thing I had in my defense was an herb I slipped into a wine bottle I was saving for my husband, who I hope to find when we arrive in Kaffa."

"How is it you do not know the whereabouts of your husband?"

She paused, struggling to come up with a believable lie. "He was taken to Kaffa after sustaining an injury during battle."

"Ah, he is a soldier, then."

"Yes, Captain. I have received word he is still there."

"Since you both appeared dead, how is it Ferox did not survive?"

"After he ingested the herb, which I had not known was so poisonous—I hoped only that it would make him sleep—he forced me to drink of the wine as well. I spit most of it out."

"I see. Signora Petra, for your protection, I think it best you remain below deck for the remainder of the trip. I will personally bring food and drink to your quarters, and I will have a trusted man help you with anything else you may need when I am on duty."

She tucked the cloak closer about her and nodded. "Agreed, Captain."

"Men, continue with the burial of Ferox while I escort the lady below. If any of you go near her, I will see you removed from sea service for the rest of your lives."

As the men gathered around the body of Ferox, Petra turned away, wishing with every step she would find Lucius before it was all too late.

Even though Petra spotted land through her tiny porthole that morning, the captain ordered his men to drop sail. Eventually, she watched as another galley ship flying a Genoese flag came alongside the *Athena*. Shouts carried between the ships as the two captains relayed news. What she heard terrified her.

"Turn back, Captain, if you value your lives at all. The city of Kaffa is under siege."

"Is it the Tatar-Mongols again?"

"Yes. All trading has ceased. Kaffa is running out of supplies. They have turned us away."

"Why?"

"We are to return to Genoa immediately to request aid."

At this, Petra rushed topside, determined to find a way to make landfall. By the time she stood before Captain Gratian, the other ship was already underway. She wore her heavy cloak, which shielded her from the fierce east winds.

"Captain, I must go to Kaffa. I cannot go back to Genoa without my husband."

"You heard the news, yes? We must turn back. The city will not let us make berth at the port."

Petra glanced toward the city, calculating the distance to the docks. She heard the faint sounds of siege machines echoing over the water. She had never been in the middle of a battle, but if Lucius was trapped somewhere in that fortress, she wouldn't rest until she found him.

"I will pay you handsomely for a boat to row ashore."

"What?" He let out a great guffaw, and those around them who heard her laughed as well. "You haven't the strength to row so far."

"I do. And I must, Captain. Take my money, and I will no longer be a burden to you."

"I could not in good conscious let a woman enter into a city under siege without even a servant to protect her."

"Captain, you will either let me have your lighter, or I will swim ashore. I would much prefer the former, but if I must I will swim—" She had begun to remove her cloak when he touched her arm.

"You will have your lighter, Signora, and one man to row you."

"Sailors of the *Athena* to me," the captain yelled. When the sailors gathered on the main deck, the captain addressed them. "You now know the city of Kaffa is blocking all but supply ships as they battle under a Tatar siege."

The men nodded, anger and frustration in their eyes.

The captain swept a hand toward Petra. "This lady has urgent business in the city and needs an escort by lighter to the port. Who will volunteer?"

None stepped forward. She didn't know if it was because she was a woman, because they feared the Mongol siege, or because she rose from the dead. Or perhaps it was because she had killed one of their own.

"Extra rations for the volunteer for a full week," Captain Gratian added.

This intrigued a few of the men. Finally one stepped forward. Grime smeared his face and hands, but he was young and able-bodied, and she felt he would do well.

"Yes, Piero Biondi come forward," the captain said with a nod of approval. "Deliver the signora safely to the docks of Kaffa, and then return immediately to the *Athena*. I will give you a letter of admittance to present to the dock master if you are questioned."

The young man nodded.

"Gather your things while we lower the lighter for you, Signora Petra," Captain Gratian told her.

"I will make haste," she said, anxious to be away. By the time she had made her way back to the deck, the sailor was already awaiting her in the lighter. The seas were running heavy, and she did not look forward to the journey to Kaffa. It looked to be several miles to the north.

She slowly made her way down the ladder leading down the hull of the *Athena* and into the waiting boat below. It was an awkward business with her heavy skirts, but she made it down and plopped herself onto the wooden bench in the small lighter across from her escort.

"Are you ready, Signora?"

"I am." She looked up at Captain Gratian. "Thank you for your assistance."

Concern etched into his features, but he held up his hand to her. "Godspeed you on your journey, Signora. I hope you find your husband in good health."

She nodded and turned to her rower, Sailor Biondi. He had brought bread and two water skins, which she would, of course, leave for him. As he began to row, she studied his hard, angled features.

"Your name, Piero… It means "stone"?

"Yes, Signora, it does."

"Does your name suit you, do you think?"

He furrowed his heavy, dark brows, which reminded her so much of Lucius's eyebrows. Though obviously surprised by her question, he took a long moment to contemplate the idea as he rowed with smooth, strong strokes. She watched the movement of his muscles for a moment.

"Yes, I would say it does."

"Why?" She was genuinely curious now.

"Nothing much moves me. Of all her seven children, my mother always used to call me the steady one. Even as a bambino, I rarely cried or caused a fuss."

"You are still this way?"

"Yes, I suppose so." He paused and gazed out to sea, unable to look at her as he retreated into a memory. "There was a time when I was not at sea. When I was set to be married to Agata Caro."

"What happened?" Petra asked gently.

"She walked into the sea with a stone in her hands and never came back to me."

Petra said nothing for a moment, as she glimpsed the pain in his eyes she realized he had never shown to anyone else.

"So you took to the sea and, still, you look for the girl with the stone in her hands."

"Yes." He almost smiled, recognizing that she understood what he could not express.

"Your name has served you well, then."

"Oh, yes. I aim to captain my own ship one day. A large merchant galley, yes." His face relaxed into a pleasant smile, as if he were picturing his future ship in his mind's eye, and she was glad to distract him from his memory of Agata.

"I believe you will have your ship one day, Piero Biondi."

His tentative smile turned into a grin. "God be willing."

"I, too, am a stone. Petra means the same."

"It sounds old. Is it Roman?"

"It is."

"Where do you hail from, Signora?"

"I come from Ancient Roman stock."

"You live in Genoa?"

"For now, yes. In a year's time, who knows?"

"The captain says your husband is in Kaffa?"

She looked toward the city, where the sounds of the siege had quieted momentarily.

"I wish I knew. I heard tell of him from strangers. From Ferox. I thought it must be him, the man he described. He should have come home from his journey by now, but he has not. I seek this man in Kaffa, hoping against reason that it is my husband."

"What is his name?"

"Lucius." Merely the sound of his name on her tongue brought her to tears.

"I thought a stone couldn't feel, Signora Petra." Piero's voice was tender.

"I once thought so, too, but you and I both know a human could never be a stone. We move, we change, and the world changes with us."

Their words turned to silence, mired deep as they were in their own thoughts while they neared the city, the sounds of the battle growing louder as the forbidding Genoese fortress loomed ahead.

"Tell me about Kaffa. Have you journeyed there before?" she asked, breaking their comfortable silence.

"Yes, many times, but never under siege."

"How will I enter the fortress?"

"I fear they will not let you pass through the docks."

"If that is so, is there another way in?"

"There are six gates into the city. You will find there are two walls, the outer wall and the great wall of the citadel. You can see the outer wall there." He pointed.

"The Mongols attack from the west?"

He glanced over as his rowing brought them ever closer to the cacophony of screaming men.

"Appears that way. If you look up above, you can see some of the thirty-four towers along the outer wall. I counted them once."

"Which gate should I enter?"

"It is difficult to tell from so far below, but stay away from the north and west gates where the Tatar-Mongols are encamped."

"Stay back from the dock and state your business!" one of four haggard soldiers guarding the nearest dock shouted at them. They looked like the very devil. Unwashed, exhausted, and wretched, they eyed her with suspicion and irritation.

"The lady's husband is in the city. She wishes to reunite with him."

"No docking allowed, sailor. Go back the way you came," the guard retorted with terse vexation.

"I plan to return to my ship after the signora disembarks."

The guard trained his piercing stare upon her. She did not look away. She stood in the boat and held out her hand to him in a show of peace.

When he caught full sight of Petra as she lowered her hood, his surprise at her beauty left him momentarily speechless. She didn't have time for such foolishness. She waved him forward, not taking no for an answer.

The guard frowned but moved to assist her. "You may disembark momentarily, Signora."

Once the guard had helped her out of the lighter, she turned to Piero. "I thank you kindly, Signore, for your assistance. And if I may tell you something before you go…"

Piero leaned over the paddles and waited.

"Don't look for your Agata in the sea. Her stone has already descended far into the deep, and she is finally at peace. You will be a captain one day. Do everything you must to keep your eye on your rising dawn in that distant horizon."

Piero nodded and crossed himself. "May God be merciful and help you find your husband, Signora."

She bowed her head toward him in thanks. And then she turned toward Kaffa and war.

III

The Horde

Kaffa, Crimea

August 13, 1346

"Now what do we do with you?" the Kaffan guard said, a mix of amusement, annoyance, and lust in his voice.

"Would you escort me to my husband?" Petra asked.

All the guards laughed at her.

"The people here call him the Immortal."

The guards sobered immediately.

"You know of him, then?" she ventured, realizing they actually feared this man. Certainly, if they had seen Lucius in the flesh, he would seem otherworldly and intimidating. In the fading light of dusk, she saw the glimmer of suspicion light their eyes. For the briefest of moments, she faced the guard without knowing how to proceed. Then she stood up a little taller and put on her most genuine smile.

"How thoughtless of me. You are duty-bound to guard the docks. I will go myself. Will you direct me toward the safest route?" She had already noticed there were multiple paths up the hill.

"Why have you come here, woman? We've a battle underway. The Great Mortality has claimed countless lives in the city of Kaffa. To go this way, Signora, is to court death."

"You speak of the Pestilence coming down from the Golden Horde?"

149

Another guard nodded, as the first guard looked at her incredulously. "You knew of it, and still you came? I ask again, woman: why have you come here?"

Petra looked in his eyes and judged him to be a decent man. "In truth, I do seek my husband. He is overdue to return home. I heard merchants in Genoa talk of a man who seemed to be untouched by pain. He is like such a one. I came because I heard of the Pestilence, and I heard of the siege. I wanted to tend my husband if he had taken ill."

"You were a fool to come. Your husband is likely already dead. And I would be a fool to let you in. Save yourself, woman. Go up into the hills east of the city. There you can wait until either war or death takes Kaffa."

"Signore, I beg you to reconsider—"

"Be gone with you before I run you through myself, Signora. I don't suffer liars or fools."

Petra stood for a moment longer, wondering if she could take all four guards on the dock before they stuck a sword in her belly. But if they killed her, she'd be thrown in with the dead corpses within the citadel. All well and good until they burned the bodies. If she did not wake in time… It seemed unlikely to her that even she could withstand a death by fire, and she'd rather not find out on this night.

"I would thank you, Signore, but you have been most unhelpful."

He touched his sword hilt and waved her away as though she were a pesky insect.

Petra stared up at the hill above them and chose a circuitous path to begin her trek west of the walled city. She passed many on her way up from the docks. She kept her face fully covered, and though her fine clothing likely hinted she was of some importance, no one accosted her. Those who shuffled past her were all unwashed men smelling of death. Their faces spoke of profound exhaustion and despair. The battle must have gone on for many long months. She had seen those expressions before, on men whose fear of battle had faded into an acceptance and desire for death. Did Lucius wear that same expression somewhere within the citadel? How would she ever find him amid the thousands of grime-smeared faces in Kaffa?

She hurried up the path, and when she was level with the main city's outer wall, she finally glimpsed the immensity of the Tatar-Mongol army out beyond the makeshift neighborhoods outside the fortress walls. The light of the day was almost gone, but she was able to make out a Mongol encampment of thousands at the outskirts of the city's outer wall and reaching all the way up into the northwestern hills.

The dark of the sky pouring over the grasslands surrounding the encampment and fires burning among the city's fortified towers gave more of a sense of oppression than the bodies of the dead scattered across the landscape. She had seen the face of war before, but she had never stood between two armies, hoping to breach the walls of a city that did not want her.

Lightweight siege machines—mostly what appeared to be a smaller form of the trebuchets and catapults she was used to seeing in France and England—stood at the front lines. Ballista also stood at the ready just out of firing range of Kaffa's outer defenses. The walls were blackened and broken from the Tatar-Mongols' offensive, but they seemed to have held fast against a breech.

Petra saw no immediate way to avoid at least the outskirts of the Mongol army on her way toward the nearest city gate. So as she watched the army slowly prepare for another assault on Kaffa, she formulated a plan. She would have to act quickly. Spying a massive pile of abandoned Mongol corpses not far from where she stood, Petra hurried toward them, the stench overwhelming her even from this distance.

Once she made her way across the rock-strewn, grassy hill, she covered her mouth and nose as she searched for a fresher body among the corpses. She found one on the south side of the pile. He lay in the mud at the foot of the tower of death and still had freshly drying blood stuck to his hair from a head wound, but his soldier's uniform looked mostly untainted. As several rats ran by her feet, no doubt ready to feast on this endless supply of corpses, she worked quickly to unclasp his cloak and roll him over to release it from his stiffening body. She was as careful as she was quick. The last thing she wanted was to have the mountain of bodies to topple over and bury her.

A moan escaped from the pile. She jumped to her feet, dropping the cloak into the river of blood at her feet. A morbid curiosity took her to the opposite side where a man lay near the bottom. Though yet alive, she knew he was not long for the world. The Pestilence had eaten through his blackened fingers and his neck was swollen with egg-shaped protuberances. He reached out to her, his eyes a mix of sheer terror and pain. Though she was fluent in eight languages, he spoke in a language foreign to her. But she didn't need to know. He was asking for help. She had none to give, save a swift, merciful death.

"It will be over soon, warrior," she whispered. "Dream now of riding horseback in the Land of Endless Blue Sky, and it will be so." And then she held her hand over the crown of his bare head and drew his life. She was quick and she was sure, and she felt at once both the weakness of his disease-ridden body and the power of his strong, clear mind.

Before he died, she caught a glimpse of the dream she had given him, and she felt herself riding bareback on a long-maned Mongolian horse in the summer sun, the green grasses beneath her horse's hooves a stark contrast to the white-cragged blue mountains surrounding a peaceful valley. Then the momentary image of paradise faded into the darkness of putrid death, and her whole body shook with disgust. But she kept to her feet and moved back to pick up the cloak that had fallen in the mire.

She heard voices as a group of men approached. She made her way around the back side of the wall of corpses, and having cloaked herself with the dead warrior's clothing, she walked sure-footed across the plain. No shouts of alarm greeted her, so she moved toward the outskirts of the encampment, hoping to avoid the stares of both the living and the dead.

As she strode through the deserted, blood-soaked neighborhoods outside the city between the Mongol horde and the Kaffan defenders, she questioned her own sanity. What was she doing here? How had her worries taken her so far from home? Lucius was likely not in Kaffa, and yet she could not stop her feet from moving into one of the most dangerous places she could possibly be. While she no longer believed in the old gods and goddesses of her Roman youth, neither did she hold with the new God either. But she had been around long enough to know there was no such a thing as coincidence. She knew there must be a reason she found herself in this godforsaken land, and she would follow where her heart led, consequences be damned.

A man shouted at her in the Mongols' strange language. When she turned, a small group of well-armed Mongol warriors approached from a muddied side path between houses, some who held scimitars at the ready and others who stood with bows drawn. One held up a lantern, so they could see her face.

Petra didn't want to know what those arrows would feel like pummeling her chest, so she held up her hands in surrender. They simultaneously shouted at her and talked among themselves. The dirt and blood covering every inch of visible skin as well as the buboes on their necks told her they must be suffering from the Pestilence, but the fierce look in their determined eyes reminded her why she had never wanted to come face-to-face with the Tatar-Mongol race.

She wished she had thought to pull her knife from the sheath secured to her thigh, but it was too late to reach for it now. In order to use her only defense, she would have to get closer, so she took a step in their direction, keeping her hands up and visible. Confusion marked their expressions and their voices grew louder, but they did not halt her approach.

Knowing her accent would instantly give her away, Petra said nothing. She decided, then, to play the part of a priestess on a mission. She swept her hands around at the vast army, and then lifted her arms to the sky as she continued to move toward them. They lowered their weapons slightly, as they tried to understand her gestures. Soon, she stood facing the man who appeared to be the leader.

Over his blue woolen undergarments he was covered in a protective shield of lacquered leather armor from helmet to gauntlets. He had a battle axe tucked into his belt, and he held his scimitar blade aloft, ready to strike.

She gestured toward the nearest siege machine, one of the Mongolian-style trebuchets she had noticed earlier. She gestured slowly, making the motion of flinging something over the wall with the trebuchet. She was merely trying to confuse them and give herself more time to formulate a plan. Then it hit her. These men were not educated in European ways. They knew war and power and little else. They had never seen magic. And that was how an Essentian draw would appear to them. She knew it was a risk. They would either shoot her full of arrows or back away in awe. Her chances weren't great either way.

The leader grabbed hold of the dead soldier's cloak around her shoulders and studied the fabric. He seemed to be angry to find a foreign woman wearing a Mongol warrior's clothing. Then he pulled down the hood of her own cloak. Her hair spilled down and the scarf covering her face fell away. They all gasped. Likely it was her immortal skin and eyes, which, in the lantern light, would appear to be glowing with eternal youth. As the leader stepped back, Petra boldly stepped forward, matching him pace for pace. With a swipe of her hand toward his chest, she began an Essentian draw of his heart.

All the men began to back up and shout, but they did not move to take her down. The leader's face moved from sudden shock to what she had hoped for: pleasure. Though she was deep within the throes of the draw herself, she forced herself to look at the other men, catching their horrified stares one by one until she knew all of them had succumbed to her show of power. And she *was* powerful. She now had the mental acuity of the man she had already drawn from and this man before her, who, despite his haggard appearance, was still strong as well as strong-willed.

She felt as though she could conquer their whole army with the flick of her wrist, but even as she felt the man's life diminishing, she knew it was a foolish thought. For a moment, she considered letting him live but decided it would be too cruel. She already knew he was beginning to experience the effects of the Pestilence. She saw it in the ashen pallor of his skin. When she felt him die, Petra caught his heavy body in her arms and gently laid him in the mud at her feet. Then she made a random sign with her hands over his body, as if blessing him, and then bowed to the men, not knowing what else to do.

They showed expressions ranging from shock to horror to reverence. She gestured that she would walk to the city gate, and they did not stop her. For a few steps, she faced them as she backed away, and when they did not approach her or raise their weapons again, she finally risked turning toward the city. For a thousand agonizing steps, she made her way across the dead zone between the camp and Kaffa's outer wall, believing that at any moment, she would feel an arrow slam into her back, but the Mongols did not pursue her. Perhaps they thought her their champion come to destroy the Genoese of Kaffa. Would the city let her in? She would soon find out.

IV

The Immortal

"**H**ALT!"

Petra froze mid-step. She had kept her eyes on the towers on her long walk to Kaffa, and no one had appeared to shoot her dead. But suddenly there were dozens of bowmen pointing their arrows down at her. And, even now, she heard the cacophony of the Mongol army mobilizing behind her. Their voices grew louder and the din of their siege machines creaked against the coolness of the night.

"I am a citizen of Genoa," she shouted up at them. "I seek a man the Kaffans call the Immortal. Please let me enter."

"You wear the cloak of a Mongol warrior, woman," a young, thin man called down from the top of the wall. He seemed to be fairly healthy and his voice was clear.

"If you will allow me to remove the cloak, I will show you I wear the fabrics of a true Genoese. I wore this Mongol cloak to ensure safe passage through the Horde."

"Permitted. Hold your fire, men!" he called across to his fellow bowmen. They lowered their arrows while she flung off the putrid cloak. She even tossed aside her own black cloak despite the chill seeping into her skin from the cold winds that had whipped up.

"A true Genoese citizen respectfully requests permission to enter the Great City of Kaffa."

"Why do you search for the Immortal, Signora?" he asked. "What

155

business have you here?"

"I am his sister," she blurted out. "I wish to reunite with my brother."

The man hesitated, deliberating.

"Do you not understand we suffer the Great Pestilence here in Kaffa?"

"I am aware, but I am immune to this illness." He stared at her in obvious surprise. He stroked his straggly beard a moment longer, and then nodded.

"Guards, raise the *portcullis*!"

"Thank you, Signore," Petra said, with a deep bow of thanks. "The Mongols are preparing to launch a new attack. Make ready!"

A few moments passed. Petra breathed out the breath she had been holding and relaxed her white-knuckled fists. The massive iron-woven portcullis heaved up with a powerful groan. The moment she could duck under the gate, Petra slipped through and found herself in a wasteland of death and decimation.

The first thing she noticed was the smell. The mangled and rotting corpses of both Tatar-Mongols and Kaffan guards lay everywhere, reminding her in hideous detail of the day she had walked through the courtyard of Clarius's villa littered with the bodies of slaves. Not even the billows of acrid smoke from dying fires could penetrate the stench of the dead in the broken city of Kaffa.

The area inside the portcullis was deserted, save for the few men manning the gate. The majority of the forward defenders were either lining the massive walls, resting amid the gutted houses, or sitting in the narrow city streets, waiting for fire or death. They looked no better than the gutter rats scurrying past them. The colors of what she knew were once fine uniforms were now the color of mud. Some of them moaned or screamed from injuries. Others she knew had already contracted the Pestilence and were starting their slow decline into the oblivion of death.

She wondered briefly whether the Mongols had climbed the walls or had somehow breeched the gate. The dead gave no answer, so she hurried on toward the maze of narrow streets beneath the watchful eyes of the tower guards above her.

Thousands of closely built houses cluttered the land between the outer wall and the inner citadel of Kaffa. Many of them were still on fire from the last Mongol attack. Others poured plumes of black smoke from previous onslaughts.

She slowed her pace as the oppression and disillusionment of the men seemed to infect her own spirits. She stopped near a group of them and addressed a man who seemed less ill than the others.

"Pardon me, Signore. I seek the man they call the Immortal. Do you know where I might find him?"

At first he stared at her as though he were dying of thirst and she was the only cool cup of water in the city. She figured he probably hadn't seen someone so healthy and clean in months.

He finally shook his head. "The rain of Pestilence is coming, Madame," he said in French. "Seek shelter before they kill you where you stand."

Petra glanced back toward the gate, but there were no arrows falling from the sky. Then she realized that by the time she heard or saw them, it would be too late.

"Incoming!" a shout came from behind. She looked back, and to her horror, it was not arrows or even ballista raining down on the city of Kaffa. It was the corpses of the Tatar-Mongols. Dozens fell all around her, hurled against the stones of the streets and the houses, limbs torn to pieces, heads rolling away from their bodies.

One corpse fell at Petra's feet. He was just a boy, no more than fifteen or sixteen, and yet he wore the uniform of a soldier. At impact, his body, swollen and lumpy from the ravages of the disease, burst open, his blood splattering the length of her skirt. She didn't even know she was screaming until a man nearby shouted at her to quiet down.

Petra fled deeper into the city, her own footsteps echoing across the dead and smoky landscape as she fled into the maze, hoping to outrun her fear that she would never make it out of Kaffa alive.

As Petra neared the main gate to the citadel, she noticed it lay open, which surprised her until she realized a caravan of death carts had just been driven through. She saw the last of them heading off to another section of the outer city. She slipped through the gate without anyone noticing. There were few people here. Those that were lay scattered along the street, either dead or nearing death. She asked a Genoese woman sitting on a stoop singing a quiet song to herself whether she knew where to find the Immortal. At first the woman did not acknowledge Petra. She was sniffing at the metal pomander around her neck as she shook it. The tiny iron ball smelled strongly of the cinnamon and clove encaged inside. It was no wonder; the woman was surrounded by the putrid bodies of the dead and dying.

"Please, Signora," Petra asked again. "I need to find this man. It is a matter of life and death."

"Immortal death you seek…?" She looked confused for a moment, rubbing her tongue across her bare gums where her teeth should have been. "You find in cathedral," she replied in halting speech, waving her hand in the direction of a massive building with a high steeple that appeared unmarred by damage or fire. She didn't think the woman had understood her, but the church seemed a beacon to her in this sea of misery. She found herself heading toward it, unsure what she might find.

When Petra finally wound through the even narrower streets near the church, she noticed a mass of people sitting in the piazza surrounding the limestone building. Some were wailing with their faces to the sky. Others knelt in the mud, eyes closed, fists clenched in prayer.

She hadn't stepped foot inside a church for many years. While she might not fear the God of the Catholics, she often wondered what their God would make of her. Many centuries past, she once honored the goddesses of her foremothers. But the Roman and Greek gods and goddesses had never answered her prayers. Yet, even despite this, she kept to some of her old ways when performing the Vellessentiae rituals. It was her way of honoring her mother's sacrifice.

Shaking her musings from her mind, she found herself with her hand on the massive, carved door of the church. Would she find her lover in there? Or would it be a stranger?

The cathedral was dark. Lit only by votive candles in the nave alcoves far ahead, the building was cavernous and forbidding. The cold and the eerie sounds of moaning and whimpering raised the flesh on her arms. The scent of blood and death hung thick in the air. As she walked further in, her footsteps echoed on the stone at her feet, making her cringe. She wanted to call out to Lucius. Could he be here? Why would he ever come to a place like this?

"Lucius?" she said quietly, hoping he would come rushing from the shadows and fall into her arms. No answer echoed through the nave. Her voice had even silenced the moans of pain. As her sharp eyes adjusted to the light, she saw more detail as she moved through the center aisle. Bodies, dead and alive, lined the walls. The smell was stronger as she approached the transept.

Petra saw a man dragging something from one side of the transept to the other. The glint of a blade in his hand caught in the light of a single altar candle. She froze.

"Lucius?" she called again, loud enough for the man to hear.

"Wait your turn, woman," the man's raspy voice ground out, though not unkindly. He pointed with a blackened finger toward the North Transept and continued on toward the south end.

This man was not Lucius. That was for certain, though he did have Lucius's height if not his lithe build. She debated whether or not to follow the man's instruction. She could draw him if he threatened her, so she did not fear him. She decided to do as he bid her, hoping the man might help her find Lucius.

When he returned, she took a better look at him. He had long hair of gold, but it was knotted with grime, and his beard was unkempt and long. Dried blood as well as all manner of cuts and bruises marred what she knew had once been a beautiful face. The Great Mortality had touched this man's body, the clearest evidence being his black-skinned fingers and nose. He looked as if he should have died already, and yet, here he was walking toward her with a sure step and determined eyes.

"What is it you seek, woman?" he asked gruffly, though his eyes belied his shock at her beauty and good health. "You seek death even as the Pestilence passes you by?"

"I seek the Immortal."

The man laughed, as blood seeped from his mouth to run a new river into his beard.

"God would not even suffer an immortal to live through this misery. Perhaps I am the one he punishes most of all."

Petra held up her hand to him. "You? You are the Immortal of Kaffa?"

"The fools who know no better call me such. Only fools or the desperate come to this church of the dead, woman. Which are you?"

"I am a true immortal, Signore," she confessed, though she had never uttered those words in the presence of another human in the whole of her long history. "I seek another of my kind. Do you know the man named Lucius Valerii?"

The man stood speechless for several long moments, while the blood from his dagger dripped to the stones beneath his bare and blackened feet.

"I have never heard the name. I am Sandro Vincenzo, and I hail from Genoa."

Her hope fell at her feet, into the blood running between the stones. Her journey had been for nothing.

"The Immortal," he muttered to himself. "I will perish with the rest of these poor, deluded souls, and I will not even feel the moment of my death. If that is immortality, I don't want it."

"What do you mean, Signore? I know intimately of death. You will feel it when it comes."

"I was born without pain, Signora, and I will die as unfeeling as I came."

"You speak the truth? Your body feels no pain?" she asked.

He nodded, his bitterness evident in his mocking eyes.

"It does not."

"And your mind?"

He mused for a moment. "Only regret. And only then for one regret alone. For all others... I feel nothing."

Petra stepped back from him, studying him from crown of head to blackened toes. Could she save him? A man who felt no pain would make a singularly useful guard and warrior against Clarius when the time came. He could even help her save Lucius during the punishment ritual Clarius had demanded.

"Do you wish to live?" she asked.

"No," he said without a hint of emotion. "I wish this Pestilence to wash away my regret so there is nothing left of me."

"Why stay here in the dark, then? Why not go out and face the Great Mortality—or even the Mongols—with honor and courage?"

"Because it is in the dark that these people wish me to hasten their deaths. They call me the Immortal, but I should have been dead long ago. I linger on to end the suffering of the children."

Petra looked on in horror as she realized the dead in the nave were mere children. The dagger Sandro held was the instrument of their execution.

"In a house of God?" she whispered. "Have you gone mad?"

He looked at her quizzically. "It is their families who bring them here to me. They cannot bear to watch the slow death of the Great Mortality. So I give them what they seek before they themselves succumb. They call it a mercy. I call it passing the time."

"You must come with me, Sandro. Into the light—and back into life. You must come away from this darkness."

"I desire the dark. And I have one more life to bring into the eternal light, so if you will pardon me..." He stepped away from her, walking toward the North Transept once more, to a girl who lay in a silent corner, her eyes closed to the shadows surrounding her.

"No, you must not," Petra said, her voice low but insistent.

"This girl is not unknown to me. She is my goddaughter and the only child of my greatest friend. I will not let her suffer any longer."

"No," Petra whispered, her heart moved by the girl, who might have been an angel if not for the Pestilence wracking her body. She walked toward them both, as Sandro lifted the girl in his arms, his dark fingers gently touching the fevered, red skin of her cheek.

"Anna, your father bid me save you from any more pain. Do you wish to fly to the angels now? To see your father and mother again?"

The girl could no longer speak. Even her nod was barely perceptible. Petra had seen such sickness before. It would not be long. Sandro brought the dagger to the girl's neck, but no emotion touched his eyes or stayed his hand.

"Stop!" Petra screamed, her voice echoing around the cathedral's cavernous dome.

Sandro withdrew the blade and looked up at her, surprise and confusion battling within his eyes.

Petra fell to her knees at his side. "Let me save you." Then she looked at the girl. "Let me save her."

"There is no salvation from the Pestilence."

"There is. I alone can offer it. But I am not in the business of redemption, Sandro. Survival is my life's work. I am giving you an eternity in exchange for service to me. Take it, and redeem yourself."

"I am not the man you were looking for. Why would you offer such a gift to a dying stranger? To one who could never repay?"

"You will repay for more years than you can possibly count. I offer you the gift of your name. And a place at my side. You must say the word, Sandro. You must say, 'I accept.'"

He moved to speak, and then he let the girl fall away from him as blood poured from his mouth. He choked and his stomach heaved as he bent over. No pain touched his expression, but she saw in the involuntary movements of his body that he was gripped in the clutches of death.

"Say it! Say the words."

But he could not. He collapsed onto the stones and choked on his own blood as the girl lay beside him, watching with horror.

She leaned down to whisper into his ear as his breathing slowed. "I will say it for you. Tonight, you will become an immortal. You and Anna. You will be beholden to me for all time. But first you will drink of true death before you will find your resurrection in me."

Petra unstoppered the phial at her neck and poured half its contents into Sandro's mouth.

"I rename you Cassian Ferro. You may be made of iron, but your soul is as hollow as a shell. I will fill you up with time, time to erase your regret."

Then she took the girl's head in her hands, whispered to her of grace and beauty and a release from the pain, and then poured death into her mouth. "And, you, sweet girl, I will name you Nencia Dolcetta. Sleep now in sweet repose, and when you wake, I will take you far from here."

When it was done, Petra collapsed against the stone wall of the cathedral beside them, horrified by what she had witnessed.

"Lucius, my love, come back to me," she whispered into the dark as her new immortals shook with the death rattle that would soon lead them back into the light.

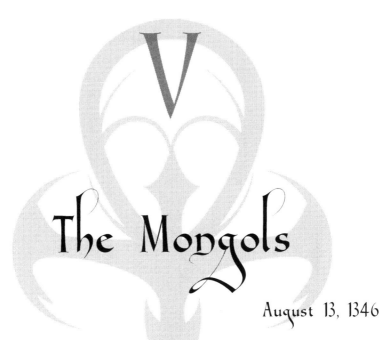

V

The Mongols

August 13, 1346

Petra awoke to the sound of faraway screams and the burning stench of smoke. She opened her eyes to a shock of daylight streaming through the rubble of stone and glass surrounding her. For a moment, she had no memory of where she was or why she lay unable to move on a cold stone floor.

Her first thought was Lucius. Where was he? Why wasn't he here to steal her away home? Then the truth hit her in the thousand images floating before her. Lucius was nowhere to be found. She had just killed Cassian and Nencia. The Mongols must have snuck in or breached a gate and firebombed the church sometime in the night, trapping them all inside.

She had not fed Cassian or the girl her blood before the ballista hit the church. They remained dead on the stone floor near her, lying just out of reach. She had never attempted to resurrect anyone so many hours after death—not even her test rats.

Raising her head to see further into the gloom, she saw at once how dire her circumstances were. The smoke was emanating from the bodies of the dead burned beyond all recognition. She was trapped under a slab of limestone the size of a death cart. Cassian and Nencia looked to be undamaged from the fallen rubble, but they might as well be on the other side of the world. One of the bodies near them still smoldered, and the smell of burnt flesh made Petra recoil and lower herself down to the putrid stones again.

Through the holes in the rubble, she was able to peer down through the church's nave. Only the roof above the apse and transepts had caved in. The way back toward the door was blessedly clear of debris. Petra felt around the stone trapping her to the floor, wondering if she had the strength to lift it. She had far superior strength to humans, but that didn't mean she had the strength of the gods in her limbs. There was nothing for it but to try.

More shouts and screams erupted in the piazza beyond the far door. Petra added her own voice to the cacophony as she pushed against the stone holding her captive. Her muscles screamed along with her as she strained against the burden. She held her breath and pushed even harder, slowly clearing a space for her legs to slip out from under the stone. They seemed to be pinned but she was able to pull them free. When she let go of the stone, it slammed down with a boom that would have woken the old gods if they still slumbered after all this time.

Some of the shouts outside quieted as Petra pulled herself over to Cassian and Nencia. She took hold of the dagger strapped to her thigh and slit her wrist. She pressed on the wound to force the blood to flow, and then she parted the girl's mouth and fed her as much as she dared, hoping the extra amount would be enough to wake her from death. She did the same with Cassian.

As she gave him life, she studied his features. How he had survived this long, she had no idea. His body was riddled with new and old injuries: an open gash and darkening bruise crisscrossing his forearm, reddish skin surrounding a nasty gash above his left eye, toes as black as his fingers, and horrible burn scars covering his right hand. She pulled back his blood-soaked, half-torn shirt and found a strange, circular scar above his breast as well as three sword and knife wounds on his shoulder and midsection.

"In this, at least, Cassian, I can help you," she whispered. "You will soon have skin as velvety as a child's." She smoothed the matted hair away from his face. "But you alone will have to heal the wounds of your mind."

Petra regretted not having drawn him. She wanted to know more about this stranger. She wanted to see the memories of a man who could feel no pain. She wished she had that gift. If she had, she would not still fear the bite of Clarius's fangs.

When she felt he'd had enough, she ripped a thin strip of cloth from her skirt and knotted it around her wrist to staunch the flow.

A loud bang resounded through the nave. Voices echoed from the narthex, voices in the Mongolian tongue she had heard uttered outside this city's very walls. The Mongols had, indeed, breached Kaffa's walls.

Petra looked down at Cassian and Nencia, realizing their deaths would keep them safe. From her limited experience turning immortals, she figured they would wake when their bodies desired it—if they ever woke at all. It could be a single hour or a day, for all she knew. She, however, was far from safe. Glancing around quickly, she realized there was no exit, save the way she had come. It appeared three Tatar-Mongols now stood between her and escape.

She pulled herself deeper into the shadows beneath a large statue of the Virgin Maria and slipped her dagger as well as Cassian's beneath her skirts on either side of her. Then she waited, attempting in vain to calm her breathing. While she might have skill with a blade, it had been many months since she'd practiced with Lucius, and she had never faced three foes alone before.

As they approached, she heard them kicking rubble aside and shouting at one another. When they entered the transept, she closed her eyes and decided to play dead. She kept her hands on the knives and practiced shallow breathing.

The men's voices were tinged with confusion. Perhaps they couldn't understand how the bodies had been set afire or why those who hadn't been burned had had their throats slit. As the men drew closer, she tried to forget that the dagger she held had butchered so many innocent children of Kaffa.

Petra tried to visualize where the Mongols were located by their voices. One man was approaching the corner where she lay prone against the far wall. The two others slowly approached from behind him. A fair amount of light was streaming in through the window. Could it be shining a light on her?

The first man kicked at Nencia, whose body was pressed up against hers. When he bent down to examine the fine cloth Petra wore, his fingers pulling at the embroidered edge of her sleeve hem, she wasted no time in sticking Cassian's dagger deep into his eye and brain. He did not even cry out but collapsed over the top of her. She didn't bother to push his stinking body off. She used him as a shield as the next man attempted to stab her with his scimitar. He ended up sticking the man in the kidney. While he was busy extricating his sword from his friend, Petra pulled the blade from the man's eye and jumped to her feet, both of her knives at the ready.

The third Mongol rushed to flank her, but she didn't let him get that far. She flipped her dagger one-handed and spun-threw it from the blade, hitting him directly in the heart. The man cried out but she turned her attention to the nearest man, as his sword swung in mid-thrust directly toward her. The point penetrated her heart, but she jumped back to lessen the damage. Still, the pain shot through her chest, as blood seeped from the wound. She spun away, fell to her knees and threw her remaining dagger. She had aimed for his heart but a shudder of pain skewed her throw. It landed deep into his stomach with a sickening thud. She collapsed onto her side amid the ashes of the burned bodies floating around her, succumbing to the waves of pain as she clutched at the wound to staunch the flow.

She lay there for an hour or more, listening to the guttural cries and gasps of the Mongol as he slowly yielded to his mortal gut wound. The last thing she remembered was her own gasp for air that would not come as her heart stopped. The echo of the Mongol's cries faded into the stones around her.

VI

The Wall

August 14, 1346

WHEN PETRA AWOKE, SHE REALIZED SHE LAY IN SOMEONE'S ARMS AND that someone was moving. She opened her eyes to sunlight filtering through clouds of smoke and the now-smooth face of a living Cassian.

He looked down at her, his face a mixture of relief and irritation.

"Immortality becomes you, Cassian of Genoa."

"Cassian?" he asked.

"I have renamed you as one of my own. You are now Cassian Ferro and the girl there is Nencia Dolcetta."

The man frowned and harrumphed but didn't respond. Rather, he stopped abruptly and called out to Nencia who followed behind them, "The lady has awakened. Bring the ale. Can you stand?" Cassian asked Petra. His eyes were now a clear, bright blue-green, his face handsome though still begrimed with a spot of blood here and there.

"I don't know."

Cassian released Petra's legs and set her down more abruptly than might be customary for the woman who had just saved his life. She figured he likely would have no idea how to do such a thing, since he didn't know what pain felt like.

Petra held to him, realizing his soiled old shirt was gone, revealing clean, smooth skin, likely hastily scrubbed in one of the city fountains.

She was curious about how immortality would treat his scarred and blackened hands, so she took hold of his wrists to examine him. The black

167

on his fingertips was fading, but his burns and other scars had completely disappeared. So, too, were the sword wounds and the gash above his eye. He was a dead man reborn.

Petra glanced at the girl, Nencia, who seemed bewildered by her resurrection. She looked to be no more than fourteen now that her face was scrubbed of grime and the buboes swelling her neck had disappeared. In another life, another century, they would have been close in age. The girl's fingers had also turned almost fully from the black into a healthy pink. She had a round, cherubic face, and when the girl's dirty hair caught the filtered light of the setting sun, it had golden strands threaded through the brown.

"I see you have made a full recovery, Cassian," she said, looking him in the eyes, purposefully gauging his reaction to his new situation.

He glared at her. "I didn't ask for this."

She frowned, surprised, as she took a drink of the ale. "You were in your death throes as was the girl, Immortal. There was no more time."

"It should have been my choice." His voice was brusque, which irritated her.

"We'll discuss it later," she countered. She wasn't feeling up to a heart-to-heart about the merits of immortality, having just taken on three Mongols on her own while dying from a stab wound in the heart. "We need to find a way out of this city. Kaffa is dying. There is nothing left here for any of us." Petra tried not to remember it meant Lucius wasn't in Kaffa, that he could still be dead or in danger… that he could be lost to her forever.

"You command much."

"I saved your life, Cassian. The girl's life too. Did you truly want her to die?"

This gave him pause, and he did not answer.

"Tell me how far we are from the nearest gate." She glanced up to the towering outer walls of Kaffa not far from the street where they stood in a dismal, blood-soaked part of town outside the citadel.

He glared at her, obviously contemplating his options.

She let out an exasperated sigh. "Know this, Cassian: if I could have told you everything before you died, I would have. I would have given you a choice, but there *was* no time. I made the choice for you because I know you will be useful to me. Certainly, you can leave me here where I stand and go your own way, but you will lose the chance to discover who and what you have become. You will be a fledgling in a world you do not understand. You will eventually die without me, a death far worse than the Pestilence you leave behind. Is that what you wish?"

She crossed her arms over her freshly healed chest, feeling strangely vulnerable and apprehensive. She had not only changed their lives for an eternity but also her own. What would Lucius say when he discovered them? Was he even alive? Or was he in another city halfway around the world, dying in a sickbed of mortal wounds she could not cure?

She shook the thought from her mind, along with the painfully detailed image of Lucius reaching for her from a pauper's bed.

"We will take the same road, but I make no guarantees for the future. This girl is now my ward, so she will stay with me." He put his arm around her protectively.

"Agreed." Petra would find a use for the girl one way or another, likely as a servant in some capacity. The idea had merit. They would finally be able to rid themselves of their human servants.

"Where is the nearest gate?" Petra asked again.

Cassian pointed straight west, where the now-sinking sun still peeked over the top of the wall at them. "Close by but it's a *sallyport*."

"A what?"

"A smaller, more hidden gate with separate wooden and steel gates."

"Raised like a portcullis?"

"No, both are hinged, so we won't need to open them remotely."

"Is this sallyport well-guarded?"

"It will be guarded by several Kaffan guards. The Mongols lie in wait just beyond the wall."

Petra noticed the sword attached to his belt as well as the pack of supplies strapped across his bare back. "Did you bring our two knives as well as your sword?"

"I stopped to pick up supplies, money, and weapons. And, yes, your dagger." He pulled the trundle from his back and laid it in Nencia's outstretched hands, as the streets were too dirty with corpses and rats. There Petra saw her own travel bag, several coins, her dagger, and flint and steel among other odds and ends.

Petra slipped the blade into its sheath. She was glad to have it back. The dagger had been an ancient gift from Lucius.

Petra waved Nencia over.

"Yes, *Nobildonna?*"

"Listen, carefully, Nencia. You, as well, Cassian. I need to tell you about your new abilities. You will wield this power clumsily at first, so use your new skills only at utmost need. Cassian, give Nencia your dagger."

He followed her instruction without question. This boded well.

"Nencia, stay behind us. If you are approached, hide the dagger until the last moment. Then stab your attacker anywhere in the midsection."

Nencia's eyes widened, but she nodded. "Or the side of the head," Petra added, which made the girl's eyes flicker with disgust momentarily.

"You are now both immortals, but even after millennia, I am still testing my limits. I have been wounded and died many times before but not in all the ways possible. You are not invincible. You will feel pain." She glanced over at Cassian, then, realizing how foolish such a thing sounded to him.

"You…" she began. "Do you…?"

"Whatever magic you wielded against us did not change that part of me." His expression twisted into a strange mix of anger and profound disappointment.

"Are you certain?" she asked.

"Yes." His voice brooked no ambiguity.

"You must be on your guard, then. You have endurance beyond that of a human. You will see better, have quicker reflexes, run faster. Your body will eventually tire, though this will be many, many hours from now."

"Nobildonna?" the girl asked, her eyes belying her shock. "Do you mean to say we are not human?"

Petra shook her head and pressed her hands to the girl's arms. "You remain a human of sorts."

Nencia's eyes were a sunny mixture of yellows and light browns, and freckles dotted her nose and cheeks. She had a slight figure but had the look of a girl who had worked hard all her life. "But you are far superior to the human you used to be. So carry this knowledge with you, young one, as we escape this pestilent city."

The girl put on a brave face and nodded, but clearly, she was terrified.

"How old are you?" Cassian asked Petra.

"You wouldn't believe me if I told you."

He looked like he wanted to protest, but she stopped him, touching his arm, which was warm despite the dropping temperatures. He shrugged away from her and rolled up the sleeping mats and secured her bag onto his back again.

"You will soon have an answer for every question. But not now. Not here at the gates of hell."

Cassian nodded. "Let's go," he said, taking hold of Nencia's hand as she tucked her new dagger awkwardly into her dress pocket.

"Keep your blade out, Nencia, but well hidden," Petra warned her. "You may soon have need of it."

Petra pulled out her own dagger and flipped it a few times in her hand, getting used to the feel of it again.

"I saw three dead Mongols in the cathedral," Cassian said, as they passed by an old man driving a tired horse through the streets, his death cart reeking of decaying corpses. "You bested all three of them, didn't you?"

Petra nodded.

A flicker of awe and respect crossed his face.

"Not before the third one stuck me in the heart like a pig at a feast, however," she said, feeling unusually embarrassed at her foolish mistake.

Petra's explanation did nothing to erase his obvious admiration.

"Where did you learn to fight?" he asked.

"That story is much too long. Just know my skill is in sword fighting and knife throwing. And I can also kill in one other way. It is called an Essentian draw. It is the drawing of life from the body. You have this ability, as well, but if you attempted to use it without practice, you would become lost in the draw yourself, which would make you vulnerable to attack."

"How is such a thing possible?"

"I wish I could tell you. There is so much we still do not understand."

"We?"

"There are more of us. The man I asked you about before… Lucius…he is such a one."

"You truly are who you say you are."

"Yes, Cassian. In time, you will see I speak the truth. How long has the Great Mortality plagued this city?" Petra asked.

"Two weeks since the first bodies came over the wall."

"And one week since my parents died of it," Nencia said, her voice as devoid of life as her family.

Cassian stopped them with a wave of his hand. He peered around the corner of a house near the wall. Petra saw the outline of one side of the sallyport ahead. The gate was only wide enough for two men to walk side by side. She spotted several guards standing watch at the top of the wall.

"How many on the ground?" she asked.

"Four. And four total on the wall above. How many can you take?"

"I survived three yesterday—well, almost. No more than that. But if we can approach to question the main guard, I may be able to draw him. Can you get me close?"

"Yes."

"I'll follow your lead," she said. "When I begin to draw him, ready your sword."

Cassian nodded. "Stay behind Petra, Nencia, and watch for arrows from above."

Petra did the same, preparing herself for any eventuality.

"Guard," Cassian called out, as they approached the sallyport. "How close is the Mongol Horde to the wall?"

"Hold there!" the haggard, blood-smeared guard shouted. "Do not advance on the wall."

"I seek only information, sir. Do the Mongols approach? Are they readying siege machines once again?"

"Why do you approach with travel gear?" the guard asked, wariness tinging his words with suspicion. He was young, to be sure, but he looked to be well-muscled and well-armed, with both a sword and bow.

"We are heading to another part of the city. We heard the Pestilence has not touched the far east side."

"Go back the way you came, you fools. You cannot escape the Great Mortality."

"I know the sallyport is barred from the Mongols. I wish only to know if the Mongols advance upon us again. We have business on this side of the city before we head to the eastern gate. I wanted to know how safe it will be if we linger here for a time."

"The Mongols have many more of their pestilent dead to throw over our city walls. I do hear rumors that some have begun to retreat now the disease has decimated their numbers."

"Do you think the siege will be over soon, then?" Cassian asked, his body language relaxing, as if he were having a chat with a friend.

"Yes, a couple weeks, at most. If we aren't all dead by then."

Cassian glanced at Petra, his gaze questioning her on whether they should wait. She shook her head slightly, and he nodded.

With every exchange, the three of them stepped closer to the guard and the sallyport, careful to ensure none of the guards eyeing them circled to flank them.

Petra did not want to kill Genoese soldiers. It would be too easy for word to get back to Genoa about them. About her. But she glanced around and realized the streets were deserted. No citizen of Kaffa would be foolish enough to wait below the walls for ballista or corpses to rain down on them. No one but the guards and the three of them.

"Signore, if I may ask…" Petra said, walking up to face the guard, her smile disarming him as she raised her hand to his heart. Petra's sudden Essentian draw was so violent she knocked him off his feet. His terror forced his mouth into a silent scream. Cassian simultaneously drew his sword on the second guard, who began to rush him.

One of the Kaffan guards above shouted in a language she did not understand. She listened to all of them nocking their arrows while she poured all her energy into the Essentian draw. She rejected the man's fear, his ecstasy, and even his strength. She cared only for the fast kill. And it was over within a minute's time. The third guard had nearly made it to her when she spun away from his hard sword thrust. In her spin, she caught sight of Nencia, who had hidden within the shadow of the wall as arrows rained down on them from the guards above.

"Mongols advancing!" one of them screamed. "They are grappling the walls."

The second guard foolishly glanced up when he heard the battle cry, and it was then that Cassian sliced through the man's abdomen. He finished him off with a gash to the throat. Petra looked away before she saw his life's blood spill onto the stones.

The third guard began to recover, even as the fourth guard approached Petra from the rear. She spun the dagger at the guard in front of her, stabbing him directly in the heart.

Petra ducked when she anticipated the fourth guard's sword slicing through the air. Pivoting on the balls of her feet, she reached up to the man's face, forcing him up against the wall with another fierce draw. This time, she was a little bit weaker, but this man was far stronger. She drew from his strength to kill him faster. Eventually, Cassian thrust his sword into the man's side, quickening his death. When he died, he was near to ecstasy, as was she. They both fell: the guard to his knees, into a puddle of his fellow guard's blood, and Petra into the strong arms of Cassian as arrows rained down around them.

Cassian quickly dragged Petra into the darkened portal of the sallyport. A small, dank tunnel reeking of excrement and death led to the wooden gate Cassian had told her about. He pressed her against the wall, ensured Nencia remained right behind them, and made quick work of the wooden gate, nearly ripping it off its hinges with his newfound strength.

"Godfather!" Nencia screamed. "The Mongols." She pointed through the grids of the steel gate, and they all took in the sight of a small mob of Mongols running toward them, some with bows drawn and firing on the guards on the wall above them.

"Petra, can you fight?" Cassian asked her.

He studied her face as she bent over attempting to recover her strength. She felt like she had been running for hours.

"A few moments more."

"I have no bow to drive them back. We will have to use our blades. Nencia, stay back as far as you can. Guard our flank and stab anyone who comes through the sallyport behind us."

"Yes, Godfather."

The girl was holding her own despite her fear. Petra was impressed.

She glanced through the gridded gate again and frowned. Something seemed wrong about these Mongols, but the sun had set and the dusk had deepened. Perhaps the lack of light was playing tricks on her.

Petra rose to her feet and steadied herself. Taking up her dagger, she nodded to Cassian who worked the lock of the steel gate.

"It's stuck," he said, yanking it hard.

"Let me see." She noticed the lock had rusted shut, but she gave it a hard pull anyway. It gave way, but not enough.

"Petra, look out!" Cassian called.

She didn't hesitate but took up her dagger and stabbed at the first Mongol who had made it up to the gate. The man's cry of pain made Petra's heart stop. She would know that voice anywhere. When she looked up into his face, she knew who she would see: Lucius staring back at her from beneath the disguise of a Mongol warrior.

VII

The Flight

August 14, 1346

"Lucius," Petra breathed, though the shouts and cries around them drowned her out.

He looked no better than those dying of the Pestilence in Kaffa. His eyes had turned silver, his extremities were darkening and even the veins along his jawline were turning black. All this she saw in the gathering dusk, and yet his expression could not hold a single emotion. He seemed shocked, then angry, and then moved to pain, and all the while she continued to hold the blade she had plunged into his chest. While she had missed his heart, Petra worried she had punctured his right lung.

"Now we are even, Petra."

She reached through the gate and touched his face. Told him with her eyes she could never be sorry enough.

"Back at the Vellessentia… I didn't mean it, Lucius. I told you to go, so I could—"

"Could be with Clarius—" His words dissolved into a hacking cough, as he doubled over and spat out blood.

Petra shook her head. "No. So I could save your life. Yours and Aurelia's. Look in my eyes, Lucius. Look and see I speak the truth."

He stared into her face, his eyes never wavering from hers. She knew he wanted to believe her but something was holding him back. And, yet, he had come all this way to find her. Aurelia must have told him where she had gone. If only Petra had waited for him there. But didn't this mean he still loved her? Only love would have brought him so far. The same love that had guided her. Hope slipped back into her heart, tempting her like a drug.

Lucius finally nodded, his anger dissolving into pain as he struggled to take a breath.

"Were you here in Kaffa all this time," she asked him.

"No, Aurelia told me where to find you. I came—I came as soon as I knew."

Petra bit her lip, trying to keep her tears from blurring her vision. He came for her. He hadn't abandoned her after all.

"Move aside, and I will finish him," Cassian shouted from behind her.

"No! Don't touch him! It's Lucius."

"You've killed him already," Cassian said, dismissively.

"I will save him," Petra snapped, and then turned back to Lucius. "I'm going to pull the dagger out. Hold fast to the gate."

Lucius nodded, taking shallow breaths, his black fingers turning lighter as he gripped the steel.

Petra hesitated as the other men reached the gate. She realized they were all Genoese dressed as Mongols. She looked back at Lucius.

"Do it," he said, bracing for the pain.

She ripped it away, feeling and hearing his muscles give way. He did not cry out, but his breath came in shallow, desperate gasps.

"Do you need my blood?" she asked, wiping the dagger's blade on her soiled skirts and tucking it into her girdle by the hilt.

Lucius could no longer speak, so he nodded instead.

"Wait a few moments, and we'll open the gate. Help me yank it free, Cassian. I need to help Lucius recover."

Cassian said nothing, but took a place by her side as they both yanked the gate open with a roar. They tore it off its hinges, and the heavy steel shook the ground when it fell, causing several rats to scurry from the tunnel back into the city.

Lucius collapsed into Petra's arms, and she pulled him outside and sat him gently on the ground against the wall. The rest of the Mongol army had not mobilized beyond them. They were lighting campfires and settling in for the night, it seemed. She was grateful they hadn't noticed the open sallyport, though they likely would on the morrow. There was no help for it. At the least, the Kaffans could once again bar the way with the inner wooden gate. She focused all her attention on Lucius as she overheard snippets of Cassian's conversation with the Genoese.

Petra sliced through the side of her neck, knowing it would be easier to hide what she was doing from the men.

She knelt before Lucius and drew close, letting him see the blood spilling from her vein. "Drink, my love, and I will make you well again."

The touch of his mouth to her skin made her want to collapse against him, to feel every inch of him next to her, to scream her love for him before every human in the world. But she did nothing, nothing but let him drink his fill as she felt the drain and the press of his tongue and teeth.

"Lucius…" she said at last, "I thought you were here in Kaffa. I was desperate to find you."

He pulled away, and already the color was coming back into his face. His brightening eyes gazed into her own, and she saw that same cascade of emotions she had seen earlier. For once in her life she couldn't read him.

"I almost didn't come," Lucius said.

If he had struck her across the face, the pain of his words wouldn't have been any less intense.

"There's no time, Lucius." She made a show of not responding. In truth she didn't know what to say. "Escape must be our only mission."

"I have commissioned a ship. These men are the crew." He waved at the Genoese men watching her with curious eyes. She counted ten of them. "The *Veroncia* is anchored off shore to the southeast."

His voice was stronger now. Her blood was making quick work of the injury she had caused him. She and Cassian helped him to his feet.

"Lucius, this is Cassian and Nencia. I will tell you more as we go, but they are coming with us."

Lucius stared at them both, frowning. He even walked up to Cassian and studied his face closely.

"You are immortal," he said simply.

"Yes," Cassian said, pulling Nencia behind him as he and Petra both braced for Lucius's reaction.

Lucius glanced back at her with a questioning in his eyes.

"You did this?"

"It's a long story, but yes."

He frowned again, waited a beat, and then nodded. "Men," he said, addressing the crew in a louder voice, "We make for the *Veroncia*. Avoid engaging with the Mongols as much as possible. We fly under the cover of darkness." He looked at Petra, Cassian, and Nencia, then. "Follow me."

Silently they moved in a single line around the North side of Kaffa's walls, staying in the shadows and out of the way of the Kaffan guards' arrows. For an hour they traversed without speaking. The only question on Petra's mind was what made him decide to come find her in the end. Was it love? Or merely obligation?

177

VIII

The Veroncia

The Black Sea

August 14, 1346

PETRA WAITED BY THE *VERONCIA*'S RAIL AS THE LIGHTS OF BESIEGED KAFFA faded into the distance. Waited for Lucius to come to her. Waited for resolution that might never come. So much had happened since the night of the Vellessentia. Since he had stabbed her. Since she had banished him.

When he finally came to her, as the dawn's light touched the distant horizon and the galley ship was long underway, he pulled the blood-soaked shirt off his body and used it to wipe the dried blood from his nearly healed stab wound.

"I suppose we truly are even now. A dagger for a dagger."

His words took her back to the Vellessentia. To the moment he stabbed her. She almost gasped with the vivid reality of the memory.

"No, I didn't see. I mean, I didn't know it was you—"

"Are you sure?" He was asking in earnest.

"How can you ask me that?"

"Because I haven't forgotten what you said to me. Your words are seared into my mind forever." Bitterness edged his voice as he tossed the bloodied shirt into the sea and leaned his elbows against the railing as the crew tacked to catch the stiffening wind.

179

Petra moved to join him at the rail, but he pulled away and stuffed his hands into his pockets. She wasn't having any of that. She forced herself between him and the rail, pressing her hands to his arms until he finally met her gaze. His expression belied his anger and a despair she knew he was trying to hide from her.

"I had to make you leave, Lucius. If you had fought Clarius, he might have found a way to kill you permanently. I couldn't have lived with that."

This made him pause, but then he pushed her away to walk the length of the deck. She followed, not knowing how to make him understand.

"Do you believe me?" she finally asked.

"I don't—I don't know how."

"You either trust Clarius or you trust me. If I didn't want you anymore, I wouldn't have traveled so far to look for you. Nothing on this Earth matters more to me than your life, Lucius." She moved around him so he had to face her. She held his dirt-smeared face in her hands as she said again: "Nothing."

Lucius jerked away. "You don't think I know that, Petra? I've known for millennia. I've known it every Vellessentia when you sacrifice your life for mine. I can still taste the horror of it. But there's something more, something that no one else on Earth could ever understand because no one else has had to experience it. I live every year knowing I breathe because you give your life for me in the most violent way possible—and there is nothing I can do to save you. If I do, I put your life at risk. Don't you see?"

Lucius pressed his fist to his chest where she had stabbed him, as if he felt the ripping pain of the wound again. She wanted to pull him into her arms, to kiss his wound, to erase all the madness that had come between them.

"You don't think I dream in blood, Lucius? I remember all of it. I've lived through centuries of it."

"You're asking me to watch you die, Petra. Again and again and again. The one who loves you. The one who would give his life for you if he could. The one who would take your place on that altar if it would ease one ounce of your pain."

"All the eternae watch. It is—"

"They don't love you, Petra. Watching the one you love die is an agony you have rarely experienced."

"You know I will always rise again."

"My mind may comprehend it, but my heart never will."

"It is my gift to you. I give it freely—forever."

"I don't want you to have to. I want it to be me. I want to be the one who saves *you*. It's my duty to protect you. Yet with a single vow to our greatest enemy, you made it impossible for me to save you from pain." He grabbed hold of the railing as several sailors ran past to catch some lines, frustration evident in his tense muscles and the tight set of his jaw.

Petra looked away, then, to the morning's fading pale-faced moon. How could she make him understand?

When he finally spoke, his voice was quieter, more resigned. "It isn't the same, you know. To die or watch someone die. I have experienced both. And while the pain of my own death fades, the memory of watching you die will never leave me. It is why I have always stayed away. Why I couldn't watch as he…" Lucius squeezed his eyes shut and shook his head, unable to finish the thought.

Petra grasped his wrist and curled her body into his arms.

But Lucius pulled back and held her at arm's length. "Everything I am or will ever be, I owe to you, Petra. I am nothing without you. So when I see Clarius pulling you into a blood-ecstasy, when I see the pleasure on your face as he takes you places I cannot… it drives me to madness, to… helplessness. I cannot compete with his blood magic."

"Why would you want to, Lucius? It is a pleasure that can only come from anger, from madness, from the greatest source of pain. It lasts only moments, and then it kills me. *He* kills me. I cannot love him or forgive him. He is my ally in protecting you, but he will only ever truly be my enemy."

"Yet you bow to him and let him have his way. You force me to follow his will."

"To keep you safe, Lucius. I have no other choice."

"You had a choice back then. And you chose *him*."

"I chose you, but I also chose to protect the world against him. My blood is the tonic to his madness. You and I saw what he is capable of, the man he becomes without my blood running through his veins."

He scowled. "I have not forgotten."

"Lucius, if my death is the price of peace, then I will gladly keep paying it. For you, for Aurelia, for Cassian and Nencia. For the world."

"I don't know how to keep from trying to kill him."

"You will do it because there is no other choice."

He shook his head but did not reply.

"Someday we will have a better understanding of the nature of my blood, but until then, we will bide our time."

"What happens on that fateful day?"

"I alone will choose." Petra stopped his reply with a kiss. He tried to pull away again, but she would brook no refusal. Her kiss deepened, and his tense muscles under her hands relaxed as his arms circled her waist. He was as needy as she was, and they ignored the stares of the sailors as they let the world fall away into the background.

Petra felt the wind and smelled the sea; she tasted heaven on a tongue; and remembered the ecstasy of his sex. She wanted him—all of him—now.

"Take me below, and then take me all day," she whispered into his ear when they broke apart.

"Petra, there is…" Lucius shook his head as desire seemed to consume him. "There is something you must know. I—"

"Forgive the interruption—Lucius, is it?" Cassian asked, and Petra noticed Nencia hid well behind him.

"Yes?" Lucius snapped, which was unlike him, but Petra knew he had other, more pressing, thoughts on his mind.

"Nencia here wondered if it was safe for her to eat food. One of the sailors offered her some, but neither of us has felt hunger since—since the change."

As Lucius attempted unsuccessfully to recover his equanimity, Petra answered for him with an encouraging smile for Nencia.

"Human food will not harm you, though you will not crave it as you once did. It is not necessary for you to function and thrive."

"Thank you, Nobildonna."

"You may call me Petra, Nencia. We stand on no ceremony in the Essentiae eternae."

"Essentiae?" Nencia asked, stumbling over the strange word.

"Yes, it is what we call ourselves."

"There are others among us who call themselves the Sanguinea. They drink blood whereas we do not, save once a year."

Nencia's eyes grew round with shock.

"Have no fear. I will share everything with you over time."

"Why did you turn them?" Lucius asked.

"Cassian here feels no physical pain."

Lucius frowned. "Truly?"

"Yes. I was born this way."

"Neither hot nor cold? Not a stab wound in the heart?"

"Nothing, Signore."

Lucius seemed to shake off the last of his desire and irritation and faced Cassian full on, studying him. It was obvious to Petra he was contemplating the usefulness of such a man. He glanced at her and nodded his approval.

"Yes, I see why you turned him. And the girl?"

"There was no time. Both of them were expiring from the Pestilence. I had to choose for them."

Cassian watched their exchange coolly. He was obviously still angry with her for making that choice without his consent.

"Come, Petra. I need rest," Lucius said, and she did not miss the suggestion in his voice. He pressed her to accompany him, but she held back.

She went to Cassian and touched his arm. "The answers are coming. You and Nencia rest. Recover your strength and rest your minds. Tomorrow you will know all—I swear it."

"And if my questions disturb my sleep?"

"Let only one question occupy your thoughts, Cassian: do you want to live forever, or do you want to die? Beyond that, nothing else matters for you now."

He looked away, then, to the sea, and she left him to his thoughts and followed Lucius below.

When Lucius pulled Petra inside their cabin, his kiss moved from feather light to a bruising press to the burning rush of an Essential draw. It took her breath away, made her fall heavily against him. He carried her to the tiny berth and there drew her over and over, taking her to the brink and bringing her back down to herself again.

Petra let him do what he would, relaxing into the pain, the terror, the pleasure, and the sheer rapture he wrought in every nerve and muscle in her body.

"You are mine, Petra," as he released her from the draw and pressed his lips gently to hers, as he finally moved to enter her.

She flipped them over and straddled him, pressing his wrists down as she forced him to look in her eyes. "No, you are mine."

"Do you ever wish we could go back?" Lucius asked her as they lay side by side in the berth, finally sated.

"What do you mean?" she asked, rising on one elbow so she could study his face. His warm brown eyes were back, replacing the silver of his blood-need. His skin was radiant with the flush of new life inside him, and his body was strong beneath her.

"Back to where we began. Before the blood rites. Before our alliances blurred right and wrong. When Clarius was still…"

"Our enemy?"

"Yes."

"Why would you want to go back there? We were slaves. Powerless... helpless... no, I would never go back."

"Do you never have regrets?"

His words reminded her she had yet to tell him of Clarius's threat. She didn't respond for a long time, searching for the right words and finding none.

"What is it? I know something is bothering you."

"It's Clarius," she began.

"What's he done?" He bolted up to a sitting position.

"It's what he plans to do, Lucius."

"Tell me."

"He wants to punish you for breaking the eternae law."

Lucius said nothing for a time. He leaned back against the bulkhead, and they both listened to the sound of the waves and the creaks of the mast for a time.

"Has a punishment been decided?"

"Not officially, no." Petra couldn't bear to tell him Clarius had demanded his head. If it was put to a vote, Clarius could end up killing Lucius permanently. She could never allow that to happen, but she didn't truly know how to prevent it either. Could the Essentiae band together and take Clarius down?

"Will the Vindicatio take place at the next Vellessentia?"

"I believe so. I don't think I can prevent it. We created the eternae laws. Laws Clarius agreed to. To go back on them now..." She didn't need to finish. They both knew what was at stake.

"I didn't actually kill him. I didn't break eternae law."

"You know he doesn't see it that way. You threatened him, and for Clarius, that is more than enough."

"What will you do?" Lucius asked.

"I don't know. I will do what I can—what I must."

"If it comes to it, Petra, I would give my life for you. That and more."

Petra shook her head. "Even I don't know what to expect from the coming Renascentia. All I know is I've traveled far to find you. I will not give you up so easily this time."

"There are centuries upon centuries of history between us all,"

Petra said after they had rejoined Cassian and Nencia on deck later that day.

The summer winds buffeted their bodies and the sun kissed their faces. Cassian seemed wary while his young goddaughter stared openly at all of them, likely attempting to make sense of her strange new life.

"Relations between the Sanguinea and Essentiae have been fraught with anger and revenge from the beginning. Our prejudices run deep."

"And you would bring an innocent child into such a dangerous environment?" Cassian countered.

Petra narrowed her eyes at him. "Need I remind you that you held a dagger to her throat when I first met you? Do not preach to me of danger. Your goddaughter is safer than she has ever been in the whole of her life."

Cassian grumbled and held tighter to the girl, who tucked her head into the crook of his elbow as they stood side by side.

"No, I didn't want to turn one so young. But I, myself, was eighteen when I became an immortal. We will do our best to protect her."

"How, if we are to attend these Vellessentiae, as you say?"

"I cannot protect her from all of it, but we will all work together. The time is coming when she will no longer be a child. We will explain as best we can why our lives are the way they are."

"Petra tells me you still have a choice before you on whether to join us or not," Lucius said. "Have you decided?"

"Choice?" Cassian nearly shouted. "What choice did I have? You think I would..." he glanced down at Nencia and pressed his lips to the crown of her head. "No, there is no choice before me. I will do this—for her and for no other reason."

"What choice, godfather?"

"To keep you safe. I will always keep you safe, my child."

IX

The Vindicatio

August 13, 1347

"I DEMAND HIS DEATH, PETRA." SHE KNEW BY THE TONE OF CLARIUS'S voice he would not yield, that he would force his Sanguinea to side with him. His mouth flattened into a hard line and his blackening lips curled into a scowl. He looked like a demon to her, with flashing silver eyes and ash-blackened skin, a walking corpse among the beautiful immortals who surrounded the cella pool.

Petra locked gazes with Lucius, and for a moment, she didn't know how to proceed. She studied his face, thought about a life without him, and then she fought.

"Lucius did not harm you, Clarius. He has broken no law."

"That bastard intended to kill me. You all saw it." Clarius wildly waved his arm around at his Sanguinea, looking less like a man and more like a rabid dog.

"And, yet, he did not," Petra replied firmly.

Clarius's mouth turned into a hideous grin, his fangs bared. "Ah, yes, but he murdered you."

"By accident!" she shouted. "It wasn't murder. It was—"

"You can't have it both ways, woman. He intended to kill me, but he succeeded with you. There is a price on his head only he can pay. I call a vote, which you know you cannot now refuse."

"I do refuse. I refuse this entire Vindicatio. You are a madman, because you walked away from our Renascentia last year. You have broken

187

our agreement, a bargain struck long before our laws even existed."

"How will you punish him, then, Petra?" he said petulantly, and she saw Lucius nearly go after him.

"Stay where you are, Lucius," Petra warned.

Clarius immediately trained his cold eyes on Lucius, but his words were for Petra. "Putting your attack dog to heel, I see."

"What I say to one of my own is not your concern, Clarius."

"It is!" he screamed, his anger getting the better of him. She was surprised he had controlled himself thus far, but if she wasn't careful, he would snap. "Everything you do affects me. Everything you do for him is a step against me."

He wasn't wrong. Of course she was working against him. She always would, until she finally defeated him.

"I call a vote!" he shouted, circling the column that held the torch throwing shadows across his face. "Begin the proceedings, Nicon."

"A punishment has not officially been put forth—" Nicon protested, his voice as calm as his master's was agitated.

"His punishment will be a Sanguine draw." Clarius locked eyes with Lucius, then, as he began to inch closer. "My draw!"

Lucius tilted his head strangely, as if contemplating Clarius's growing madness. For a moment there was a breathless pause, and then Lucius spoke with a calmness that terrified Petra.

"Let the vote proceed, Petra."

All of them stared at Lucius, but Petra began to realize what he meant to do and why.

"No, I can't let you do it."

"He said it himself. You cannot stop it. Now vote." Lucius gazed directly at her, daring her to send him to his death. So he could finally know what it felt like to die for love. So he could finally know what blood-ecstasy felt like.

"I vote no. No, Clarius!" Petra shouted. "Do you hear me? Damn you!"

"I vote yes." Nicon's voice was quiet but his allegiance was clear. She had hoped he would have the courage to vote against his eternae, but it was a fool's hope. She was sure Clarius had threatened all of them not to defy him.

"I vote no," Aurelia countered with a nod of solidarity toward Petra and a smile of encouragement at Lucius.

"I vote yes," Phaedra said, her voice loud and steady.

Silvio voted the same, though his momentary hesitation heartened her, but it mattered not. Cassian and Nencia were not officially part of the eternae yet, so they could not vote. Clarius knew this. They all did.

Clarius laughed, and it echoed out over the pool and around the cella. "I vote yes."

He didn't hesitate. He rushed at Lucius with immortal speed and dragged him into the pool where they fell together, splashing water onto Phaedra and Silvio.

"Don't—!" Petra screamed. But the vote was cast, the punishment agreed upon, the transgressor getting his just reward, the executioner getting exactly what he came for.

Yet she couldn't stand to watch. She waded into the water, moving toward them as Clarius grabbed hold of an acquiescent Lucius and ripped into his neck, his artery spraying blood out into the pristine pool.

Petra screamed as Lucius cried out. She moved faster, instinctively trying to pull Clarius from Lucius, but he was too strong. A moment later, Nicon was at her back, yanking her away.

"No, no! Let me go. He's killing him!"

"You must not stop this. Eternae law forbids it."

"I don't care!"

"He agreed to this, Petra," he whispered into her ear as he held her. "You will bring him back."

That made her stop, made her wipe the tears from her eyes and look at Lucius's face. Pain crossed his features as Clarius drew and drew, filling his body with Lucius's strength and skill and beauty. She ached to see it. Felt the exquisite agony of helplessness he himself had felt for millennia.

"Nicon," she breathed, "when we die, take Clarius far away from here."

He pressed his temple against hers so she could feel him nod his head.

"Lucius…" she said aloud, as the only sound was Clarius's growls of pleasure at finally killing his immortal enemy. As Lucius's pain moved into the final ecstasy before death, she held out her hand to him, though he was just out of reach. "I understand now," she said, loud enough for him to hear. "I understand what I couldn't then. I'm sorry."

Through the thick, humid air, she felt his life force leaving him, and Nicon finally let her go. She moved around the men, where Clarius had pushed Lucius hard up against the center altar. Even though it made Clarius growl again, Petra pulled Lucius up onto the stone and held tight to him. She took up his hand, which was as weak as a child's now that his strength was nearly spent. His shuddering body made her own limbs shake, and her own cries mingled with his as his life force disappeared, and he fell limp against her arms.

When she became aware of anything outside of her own grief, Clarius's laughter, guttural and infinitely cold, brought her back to the present.

"I haven't had such pleasure in centuries." Clarius wiped Lucius's blood from his chin and licked his fingers. "The taste of another immortal's power. The strength of a man this time. And now it courses in me, Petra. He bleeds in me."

"Be done with it, Clarius. Be done and leave us."

"I want you to remember this," he said, taking her roughly by the arm and dragging her across Lucius's still-warm body. "I want you to remember as I take you that your lover's blood runs in my veins. Soon, yours will too."

Clarius grabbed her neck and his fangs dug deep. She refused to cry out, refused to give him an ounce of her consent. No, she would not ever forget. She would remember this moment and this death for centuries to come. And when all was done, and she had destroyed him at long last, she would bury this memory forever.

She let the burning fire of Clarius's venom and the pain of his rough hands guide her to a strength of will that would keep her alive beyond the moment when he had had his fill of her. Even after she had drawn him into death with a vengeance matching his own. Even when she lay still as one dead and Nicon dragged Clarius away, and all that remained was the sound of running water, as it had been in the ancient days. Her lips found Lucius's mouth, and she rested there, curled next to him, feeling his warmth passing away as the night winds cooled them both. A warmth she would resurrect tomorrow with her immortal kiss.

"I understand now, Lucius," she whispered into his lips. "At last I understand."

The First Codex

Sicily

February 21, 1723

THE DAWN'S LIGHT CAME UP OVER THE DISTANT HILLS AND SHONE FULL ON the Prima Vita's face as she finished her history. The lady gazed absently at the seat where Lucius had been sitting. He had left them before Petra relayed the story of the Vindicatio. Aurelia found it strange that after so many centuries, Lucius still could not bear to revisit that ancient moment in time. And, yet, she understood. She had been there, after all, during this tumultuous time. She had seen the after-effects of their pain and their grief.

"I grow weary at last, Aurelia," Petra finally said.

"Of the past or the hour?"

"Both." She laughed softly.

"Pardonnez-moi, Madame. It cannot be easy to dredge up such horrifying memories."

"If I were like you or Lucius, my mind would surely have let those memories fade centuries ago. As an endless play in a darkened theater, my mind plays them back to me. Once a memory begins, no distraction can pull me out of it. I see it unfolding in front of me as if it were happening all over again."

"Why after so many Vellessentiae have none of us acquired your great skill for memory?"

"I do not know. To some degree, I think you all must have this ability. It's just not as transferrable as some of our other skills. I think, however, if we drew from each other more often—even every year—it would hasten the transference."

"Is that what you would wish?"

"Yes. I would have you all be the best versions of yourselves that you can. Someday those shared skills may mean the difference between life and death."

"But we are immortal, Madame. Life is all we know."

"It may not always be so."

"Forgive me, Madame, but is there something I should know?"

"Oh, don't listen to the ramblings of an old woman, Aurelia. I worry needlessly about my Essentiae, so you don't have to."

"You may be on in years, but you have the face of a young Diana, Prima Vita."

"As do you. Though, I believe your new lover would call you Venus."

Aurelia blushed at this. "Cassian is not mine. As much as I…" She couldn't bear to finish the thought aloud. *As much as I would wish otherwise…*

"Ah, but I have seen the way he looks at you, Aurelia. He is in love with you."

"His strange nature… is beyond me, I fear."

"You must not fear to love him. I may chide him endlessly. He may despise me for the wrongs I have done him, but Cassian is a good man. He is worthy of you."

"Is he still angry with you over his turning? He never speaks of it—"

"Yes, the old anger lingers in his mind."

"Do you regret what you did?"

"Do I regret taking his death from him? No. I regret that, after all this time, he still hasn't come to terms with whatever demons he's struggling with."

"I don't truly understand him."

"I don't either, Aurelia. He keeps silent about a past he should let go of. I fear it will be his undoing."

"Please don't say that, Madame."

"We can never live beyond the mistakes we do not learn from. Of all the things I've learned in my long life, that would be the one piece of advice I would leave you with. Don't let him be your regret. Frankly, I've never seen a man hold a grudge longer than Cassian."

"I have, Madame."

"Oh?"

"You, Lucius, and Clarius."

"Ah." Petra's smile was sad, and Aurelia regretted reminding her again of those ancient grievances.

"If you could go back and change what happened that day, would you have let Cassian die?"

"No. I regret only that I could not gain his consent before he slipped into unconsciousness. He is and will always be a part of the Essentiae."

"Yes. I cannot imagine our lives—my life—without him now."

"Go to Cassian, then. You have listened to the horrors of our past long enough tonight. Rest well knowing you are safe within the sanctuary of my house and in the arms of one who would protect you with every ounce of his blood."

Aurelia set aside her quill and left the codex's last page open to allow the ink to dry. She blew out the candle, and the shadows of the book-shelves descended amid the rays of the sun.

Petra embraced her, and then her slight form faded into the dark-ened hall leading toward her bedroom. But before she turned the corner, she called out Aurelia's name.

"Yes, Prima Vita?"

"Give yourself body and blood to Cassian. Love him without hesi-tation, without regret. Someday the tide will turn, and this fragile peace between the Essentiae and Sanguinea… this peace will not last."

ABOUT THE AUTHOR

USA Today and *Wall Street Journal* Bestselling Author Cheri Lasota is a freelance author, editor, designer, and founder of AudaVoxx.com. Her bestselling debut novel, *Artemis Rising*, is a 2013 Cygnus Awards First Place Winner and a 2012 finalist in the Next Generation Indie Books Awards. Cheri also helped found the *Paradisi Chronicles*, a massive open-source Sci-Fi universe set on the fictional planet, New Eden. Her *Paradisi Exodus* series focuses on the early years of the human exodus from Earth to the new planet. Cheri's most recent project is her ambitious Historical Fantasy series, *Immortal Codex*, which explores the lives of immortals throughout history.

Sign up to receive news of Cheri's latest book releases via her newsletter at CheriLasota.com.

If you enjoyed *Petra*, feel free to review the book on your favorite online platforms. I'd love to hear your thoughts on the story.

Read more of Cheri's books here:

CheriLasota.com/book-table

GLOSSARY

ACHERON. One of several mythological rivers over which the souls of the dead had to pass in Hades. Etymology: Greek, Latin.

AETERNITESCENTIA. The Initiation. The act of becoming an immortal. Etymology: Latin-based. Origin: Author.

ALTARAE AEVITATIS. Altars of Immortality. Etymology: Latin-based. Origin: Author.

AMOR MEUS. My love. Etymology: Latin.

AMPHORA. Ancient vessels used for holding oil, wine and other liquids. An amphora's defining characteristics include two handles and a tapered bottom. Etymology: Latin.

ANKH. Egyptian symbol of mythology later picked up by the Ancient Romans and other cultures. Etymology: Egyptian.

ANTIQUA MEMORIA. Ancient memory. Etymology: Latin.

ARTAVUS. Original meaning: "quill knife." In the context of this book, it refers to a ritual knife. Origin: Author.

ATRIUM. An open-roofed hall near the entrance of an ancient Roman house. Etymology: Latin.

CAUL. A close-fitting, netted cap that wraps around the hair. Etymology: French.

CHARON. The mythological ferryman who carried the departed across the river Styx. Etymology: Greek.

ERA. The lady of the house. Etymology: Latin.

ESSENTIAE. Enclave of vampire immortals who kill by drawing the life essence from their victims. Led by Petra Valerii. Etymology: Latin-based; meaning "essence." Origin: Author.

ETERNAE. Enclave of immortals. Etymology: Latin-based. Origin: Author.

KAFFA. A 14th century Genoese port and flourishing trading settlement on the southeast coast of the Crimean Peninsula. Known also as Theodosia, Caffa, and more recently, Feodosiya. Etymology: Various origins.

LARARIUM. Household religious shrines in entrance halls of Ancient Roman houses. Etymology: Latin.

LATIFUNDIA. A large farm or villa in ancient Rome, typically worked by slaves. Etymology: Latin.

LUCIPOR. Literal meaning: Lucius's boy. A naming construction used for slaves. Etymology: Latin.

MA CHÈRE. My dear. Etymology: French.

MON ANGE. My angel. Etymology: French.

MORTANINE. A deadly poison made from mortanine flowers. Used for the purpose of turning immortals. Etymology: Latin-based. Origin: Author.

NOBILDONNA. Milady. Noblewoman. Etymology: Italian.

PARDONNEZ-MOI. Forgive me. Etymology: French.

PATER. Father. Etymology: Latin.

PORTCULLIS. A fortress gate made of grated wood and/or iron. Etymology: Anglo-Norman.

POSTICUM. A servant's side entrance in an Ancient Roman house. Etymology: Latin.

PRAENOMEN. An Ancient Roman's forename. Etymology: Latin.

PRIMA SANGUIS. First blood. Etymology: Latin-based; meaning First Blood.

RENASCENTIA. The Rebirth. The renewal of all the immortals by way of Petra's healing blood. Etymology: Latin-based; meaning "rebirth.". Origin: Author.

SALLYPORT. A small opening in a fortress used for making a sudden charge outside against an enemy during a siege. Etymology: French and Old English.

SANGUINEA. Enclave of vampire immortals who drink blood. Led by Clarius Avidus. Etymology: Latin-based; meaning "bloodly" or "blood-stained." Origin: Author.

TABLENUM. An Ancient Roman house's finest room. Etymology: Latin.

TRICLINIUM. Dining room in an Ancient Roman villa.

VELLESSENTIA. The Drawing. The Essentian or Sanguine draw of any immortals who wish to gain skill or knowledge from another immortal. Etymology: Latin-based; meaning to "tear out life essence." Origin: Author.

VINDICATIO. The Punishment. The act of being punished for crimes against one of the eternae. Etymology: Latin-based; meaning "avenging wrong." Origin: Author.

VOLUPTAS MEA. My delight. Etymology: Latin.